Postpone

By
Diane M. Dresback

This is a work of fiction. Names, characters, places, and incidents either are the product of the author's imagination or are used fictitiously, and resemblance to actual persons, living or dead, business establishments, events, or locales is entirely coincidental.

Published by Mindclover Productions LLC
Phoenix, Arizona, USA

Copyright © 2017 by Diane M. Dresback

All rights reserved. This book, or parts thereof, may not be reproduced in any form without permission.

GET MY FREE SHORT STORY

Join Diane M. Dresback's Insiders email group and receive a free digital short story prequel to the *Awake As A Stranger* trilogy. By signing up, you will also receive periodic notification of book releases, free giveaways, and author updates.

This short story prequel offers insight into transformative events that happened to Treaz and to Omani as children; situations that affected who they grew up to be. These two women do not meet until they are adults, but their lives are on target to intertwine in the most peculiar and fascinating manner.

The *Awake As A Stranger* trilogy follows the journey of Treaz and Omani. They reside on two different continents yet each are trapped in deplorable realities—Treaz living within other people's bodies and Omani being held captive on her uncle's compound.

Both long to regain control over their lives, escape their merciless captors, and expose the haunting truths facing them and the world. Can they find freedom together?

Get YOUR Free digital short story by visiting
www.DianeDresback.com

DEDICATION

This book is dedicated to Arlene Terri Cox (1936-2016) for her selfless, life-giving decision which allowed me a chance in this world.

ACKNOWLEDGEMENTS

Trenton Greyoak and Devon Dresback for invaluable brainstorming and feedback on *Postponement*. They have been involved since the conception of the idea which began as a 48 hour short film challenge we participated in together years ago.

Deanna and Trenton Greyoak for cover design.

Teresa Young for delineating discrepancies in my characters and my story.

Ixchel Cherandon Bogford (and her parents H. Cherdon Bedford and Brandon Bogford) for making the *Postponement* book cover her first ever modeling gig! Also, to H. Cherdon Bedford for creating the cover photograph.

Rick Silber for being the most supportive husband ever — get the fold-out table ready, honey!

My Insiders email group for your support of my writing and creative endeavors. Thanks for reading and spreading the word!

Charles and Mildred Gerg — Miss you, Mom and Dad.

"Our greatest impact on the world will be the impact we have on one another."

— Diane M. Dresback

CHAPTER 1

Blaring sirens forced morning rush hour commuters to the sides of the frontage road running along the busy interstate. Neither the passenger nor the attending paramedic noticed the rays of light reflecting off Lady Bird Lake. Morning joggers and cyclists were fulfilling their passions for exercise before the heat of the summer day set in.

"Almost there, Yvonne, almost," Mo said placing a cool hand on her sweating shoulder attempting to calm the groaning woman.

"Please hurry," came her breathless voice as she squirmed on the thin mattress.

They flew past the University Medical Center and continued to the highway entrance. A scratchy voice crackled from the radio, "Six-fifty-seven, what's your status?"

"Seven minutes out," said Kevin, the emergency medical tech, while weaving in and out of hurried morning drivers. He smirked, "Have I said lately that traffic sucks in this town?" Even with the siren's rise-and-fall resound, people took their time figuring out how to give the ambulance passage over to the fast lane of the roadway.

"Copy that. FYI. Destination reports demonstrators in the area. Proceed with caution," came the dispatcher's reply.

"Right-oh, dispatch," returned Kevin hearing intense gasps coming from the back. "I'll tell the gal in the rear to kick back and relax. Maybe peruse a gossip magazine or two." He rolled his eyes, smacked the radio off and transitioned to another freeway, happy to find less congestion enabling him to increase speed. Five minutes later he exited the highway and headed towards an upscale suburb of Austin, Texas.

As Kevin turned down another road, Mo looked into Yvonne's red eyes, trying his best to keep her focused on him. "Don't hold your breath. Deep breaths now," he said nodding his head in approval as she drew in a long inhalation and blew it out slowly. "There you go."

The ambulance turned and Kevin yelled out, "Hang on."

They came to a sudden stop. Mo held his patient's hand as her body propelled forward from the force. "Concentrate on me," he repeated. "Your breathing. In and out. In and out. Yes, good."

Kevin stared out his window at thirty or forty protesters milling in front of the driveway he needed to enter. He switched off the sirens and blasted his horn to entice the stubborn crowd to budge from his path. "Get out of the way people," he complained out loud as he raised his hands. "A fly caught in molasses," he mumbled.

Sign carriers from the mob fixed laser beam glares upon him. "Babies deserve life," they bellowed. "Babies deserve life!"

Angry people swarmed around them. Inside Yvonne jumped at abrupt bangs on the side of the ambulance, but her best friend in the world right at that moment, the stranger seated right by her side, would not allow her to become distracted.

The transport eased through the agitated group at a snail's pace. Their faces contorted in rage, their fists flailing as they chanted, "Let the babies live! Let the babies live!"

One long blonde-haired woman in her early twenties garnered Kevin's attention. She peered up at him with translucent blue eyes. Perhaps she proved more reasonable so he smiled and using his index finger indicated the back of the building. To his disappointment instead of cooperating she joined in the cries of the others, "Let the babies live!"

A skinny middle-aged woman with short blood-red hair startled him when she slammed her hand hard against his window, her twisted face an inch from the glass. "It's life, not convenience!" she screamed.

"Shit," Kevin muttered, his heart jolted into rapid pounding. He waved his arms in exasperation, "Get the hell out of my way." Tempted to nudge a handful of picketers with his front bumper, he laid on the horn. They shuffled to the side allowing him to break free of the swarm.

Kevin hastened past the massive glass block wall of the grandiose lobby. He advanced along manicured flowerbeds brimming with apricot daffodils and white hibiscus. "How's she doing?" he called out as he rounded the end of the white stoned building following the words,

THE POSTPONEMENT CENTER
PICK UP AND DELIVERY
AUTHORIZED PERSONNEL ONLY

"Excellent," replied Mo smiling down at Yvonne. "She's got this." Through a face drenched with perspiration, she simpered up at him.

Male and female nurses dressed in blue scrubs stood waiting at an open roll-up door. Kevin backed into the bay, then clamored out to unlatch the back. He and Mo slid out the stretcher as the nurse shoved forward a second gurney. With one coordinated movement, the patient transferred from one bed to the other. The female nurse lifted the side rails while her male counterpart accepted the handheld device from Kevin.

Two weeks shy of a full term pregnancy, Yvonne winced and grabbed hold of her contracting belly. She stared up at Mo for reassurance. He grinned and stroked her sweat-drenched forehead, her face puffy and rosy. "You're gonna do great." Her eyes squeezed shut and he turned to the nurse, "Contractions are two minutes apart."

She nodded and wheeled the uncomfortable woman through swinging doors saying, "It won't be long now."

"What's with the yoyos out front? Haven't seen them in a while," Kevin asked.

The male nurse consulted his watch, logged the information and touched his thumbprint on the portable tracker before handing it back. "Seventh anniversary of Placer v. Grassmen."

"Ah," Kevin nodded understanding all the excitement. "Makes sense."

The paramedics reloaded the empty bed into their vehicle and climbed in the front seats. After they pulled out, the nurse engaged a wall button causing the door to close with a faint grinding sound.

The gurney moved down a pale yellow hallway. Another one of Yvonne's contractions subsided as a woman with hazel eyes and shoulder length mousy brown hair approached. At fifty years of age, her slender figure fit well into pressed black pants and a forest green knit polo top. Her arms grasped a grey tablet tight to her chest rubbing against her company issued name tag reading,

NORA COLLINS, CLIENT LIAISON

When Nora reached them, the nurse stopped, leaned against the wall and retrieved her phone to respond to a text.

"Hello, Yvonne," said Nora with a cursory smile.

"Hi," she responded relieved to see a familiar face.

The liaison placed the tablet into Yvonne's hand, gave her a lightweight stylus and pointed to the screen. Another labor pain would hit at any moment so the pregnant woman scratched a rough signature, then paused to think.

"June second," Nora confirmed and Yvonne scribbled the date. "A little earlier than anticipated."

"Yeah and my husband's out of town."

Yvonne's head fell back and she grunted letting the tablet slip from her hands. Nora made a catcher's save before it smashed on the linoleum floor.

"We gotta go," said the nurse shoving her phone back into her pocket. She began advancing the gurney further down the hall.

Nora strode alongside, "They're going to take you into pre-op now."

Irritated, the nurse said, "All right. I think we've got things figured out."

Nora stopped walking, clenched her jaw and watched her client roll away. She turned and walked a few steps in the opposite direction stopping in front of a secured door. A slow breath exhaled from her lips, as if laboring herself. The first genuine smile of the day spread across her face.

In bold letters the placard on the door read,

CRYPOD HOLDING
AUTHORIZED PERSONNEL ONLY

Nora swiped her employee badge and heard a clunk as the lock disengaged. She gripped the smooth stainless door handle and pushed.

CHAPTER 2

As the door swung open to Crypod Holding, Nora's short-lived annoyance became pacified. The distant bubbling was music to her ears; welcoming and verging hypnotic. She entered triggering a whoosh from the pneumatic door closer. Her eyes gravitated in an instant to dozens of clear rectangular shaped crypod units lined up end to end and double stacked.

"Nora," came a brash voice interrupting the tranquil moment. "Had another 4301. File's on your desk."

Nora pressed her lips together. She loathed 4301's and didn't care for Amisha, a woman from India in her mid-thirties dressed in pale pink scrubs. The Crypod Technician scratched at a loose pony-tail of dark brown hair. She kept focused on shuffling papers at a small workstation.

"Which one?" Nora asked, a stab in her belly.

"Neonate A-255," said Amisha not looking up.

Nora shook her head. "Annie. I remember her parents."

"Well, that's what they get," Amisha said extending her arms high allowing her mouth to fall into an expansive yawn ending in an obnoxious wail.

Nora cringed, disliking the assumptive statement that implied everything revolved around money —- which it often did.

Amisha stood rubbing her eyes causing the final remains of mascara to smudge on her silky skin. She scooped up a handful of orange client folders, said nothing further and exited Crypod Holding.

Once alone, Nora's gaze returned to the crypods and she walked to the first row. Each transparent Plexiglas unit measured twenty-eight inches in length, fifteen wide and twelve deep — enough to encase a single newborn baby. Silver metallic hoses yielded an ever-circulating, fog-like appearance inside the enclosure creating a halcyon gurgle. A recessed interior LED light cast a mysterious azure blue glow as it refracted off the misty particles.

Nora approached the first crypod, leaned over and peered in. She smiled speaking in a quiet manner, "Brandon, how you doing, honey?" Through the white haze the faint outline of the newborn's body lay motionless.

"How's your neighbor, Missy?" Nora continued on still bent forward. "Beautiful as always. Spoke with your parents yesterday. Another year or so and you might be going home."

Nora greeted each of the babies by name as she moved along the line of crypods. Her joy came from those still ones and she felt the most relaxed and comfortable when she was with them. They didn't make judgments nor pressure her, they simply slept patiently waiting for the opportunity to awaken and begin living their lives, whenever that time came.

Stopping at one crypod, she gazed through the mist to the little boy encased within. He had dark curly hair and the hint of dimples in his chubby cheeks. Convinced he knew she was close by, Nora reached up and placed her fingertips on the hard, cool surface. Tears formed as they had on this day every year for the past seven. "Happy birthday, Toby." One of the salty droplets escaped falling onto the crypod and she brushed it away.

Nora sensed someone's presence and straightened up blinking away any evidence in her eyes. She turned to face a lab-coated man six feet away — Dr. Leonard Thompson, the Senior Obstecryogenist and everyone's supervisor.

Perhaps another decade before complete grey took over, he stood with his hands resting in his pockets and his shoulders pushed back. He wore a slight frown on his face. "Isn't there a training session with Risk Management starting..." he glanced at his watch, "...ten minutes ago?"

Most people liked the boss, but Nora believed that he picked on her unfairly. Of course, it didn't help getting called out on missing meetings. She was not the biggest fan of corporate policy and procedures although she did recognize the need for some of it. "Yes, Dr. Thompson," Nora managed avoiding eye-contact as she headed towards the exit. He exhaled and shook his head after her.

Nora bounded out the door running smack into the broad and solid chest of JC, one of the two guards on the premises during the day.

"Whoa there!" he said. "In a hurry?"

"Sorry, JC," apologized Nora. "Just late for a meeting." She scurried down the hallway.

CHAPTER 3

The new polyester running shorts and shirt felt light and non-clingy to Nora's sweaty skin. She wondered why she hadn't purchased them years ago. Brushing the beaded moisture from her forehead, she stopped underneath a tree and, between gasps of air, sipped from a water container. From her wrist dangled a leash attached to another panting little life that plopped her wagging rear end to the grass.

From her back pocket Nora removed a small collapsible bowl and poured in some of her water so the thirsty mutt could partake in her refreshment. "There you go, girl," she said and scratched behind Belynda's furry ears.

The running route she took most afternoons after work passed through an over-sized nearby park in her neighborhood. It always held activity with the basketball courts, volleyball nets, and a massive open grassy area where dog owners tossed Frisbees and balls while excited animals chased and retrieved bits of plastic for pure joy.

However, Nora's most favorite spot was located at the edge of the field. After Belynda had lapped every last drop of water up, Nora retrieved the water dish and began walking towards the playground.

The wiry brown and white dog attempted to stop at every bush, despite yanking and pleading. "Come on, Belynda. You can't have any more pee in you."

Soon the peak of a red fiberglass slide emerged from over the slope. A four-year-old blonde boy sat on the top with a line of kids taunting him from behind. "Hurry up!" they yelled, "Go down, go down!" But he remained stiff, unable to move. Nora watched as she advanced closer to the playground. "Get out of the way you scaredy cat." Then the chanting began, "Scaredy cat, scaredy cat. Meeeowww."

Tugging came in Nora's gut. *Stop it. Leave him alone*, she wanted to shout as she sat down on a bench.

The young boy's chin started quivering as he drew his legs up tight to his chest. He pushed back against the warm little bodies all piled up behind him wiggling around until able to descend the ladder. Running full speed, he jumped on an open swing and with ferocious pumps, he swung higher and higher.

"Hi Ms. Collins," a voice came. Nora turned to see a fifteen-year-old girl dressed in holey black jeans and a black T-shirt with lettering too faded and washed to even read. Eight rings gripped each ear and a silver circle looped through the septum of her nose.

"Molly, how are you?"

"Alright, I guess," the girl answered. She walked over and perched herself next to Nora reaching down to pet the dog lying in a sliver of shade. "Hola Belynda."

"How's your mom? I haven't seen her at Sprouts lately," Nora asked fearing the worst, again.

Molly brought her feet up and hugged her knees reminding Nora of the fear and hurt the little boy on the slide just experienced. Her fingers absently played with a healing cut on her forearm. A half dozen additional scars shined in the sunlight. "She got fired."

"Oh, I'm sorry to hear that," said Nora. Molly's mother had started working at the local market a month before. It was her third new job since Molly and her single mother had moved in opposite from Nora less than a year ago. Their residence retained the award for being the only problem house on the street — the one with more weeds than lawn, bushes overgrown and trash piling up in front of the garage door. It was also the house that boasted a steady stream of renters moving in and moving out on a regular basis under the care of an absent landlord that employed a property manager to handle the dirty work when a tenant needed evicting.

"Are you still stocking for them at night?" Molly nodded then said nothing further so Nora asked another question. "School going well?" The girl shrugged continuing to remain silent and Nora started feeling awkward. Teenagers were so hard to talk to sometimes.

After checking her cell phone, Molly entered a text then put it down by her side. With what bitten-down fingernails still existed, she picked at a bloodied hangnail. She broke the silence with a fraudulent cheeriness. "So, you like your job? I bet it's cool." A child screeched in delight as she slipped down the slide.

"Sometimes," replied Nora. Belynda barked at a couple children sprinting by and Nora reached down to pat her head.

Molly tilted her face up to the sun and closed her eyes absorbing the sun's stifling heat. "I wanna move out. Get an apartment with my boyfriend."

Nora added more water into Belynda's bowl as she searched to find some wise words to share. "What's the rush?"

"You know my mom's a waste. She screws up any chance she gets. Flunks out of on-the-job training, gets kicked out of rehab. I keep a job longer than her."

"That's a bit harsh."

"Right. I'm the kid here," said Molly observing the kids swing on the monkey bars. "Old people are supposed to be responsible, like you."

Nora exhaled. There was no reason to fabricate another picture of Molly's mother nor herself. She reverted her gaze back to the playing children. The mother of the little boy that was swinging away his anger jogged over to him calling out, "Sweetie, not so high." She caught his feet slowing down his motion. The boy wiped away a tear, sprung off the seat and ran over to a slow-moving merry-go-round. He flopped down smack in the middle, both arms folded, lower lip protruding. There he stayed sulking, rotating around and around.

CHAPTER 4

In loose pajama pants and a tank top, Nora carried an opened bottle of Chianti under her arm, an oversized glass of wine and a heaped plate into the room. Belynda trotted close at her ankles — a trip disaster waiting to happen.

Nora sat down on the couch using one foot to push aside the items on the coffee table making room for the crystal and support of her feet.

Belynda was unable to shift her steadfast ogle from the mound of noodles topped with balls of meat and smothered in delectable smelling sauce. A string of saliva stretched from her mouth as she watched Nora take a bite of spaghetti. "Uh," exclaimed Nora to the dog. "You'd think after a half century, I could make pasta that wasn't mushy."

Uninvited, Belynda jumped up and nuzzled in next to Nora. The dog's nose twitched as she inhaled the delicious aroma. It was far more appealing than what waited untouched in her own dish. After gawking at the food and Nora's face for an eternity, she knew no immediate reward appeared likely. Belynda plopped her head on Nora's thigh, let out a long over-dramatic exhale and shut her eyes.

With the weight of the small animal's head and her warm breath blowing light and rhythmic, Nora smiled delighting in the simple sensation. It was the same closeness she experienced when holding reanimated babies at work. That was why she stayed; certainly not because of the people she worked with nor her boss. It was all about the children and, of course, the chance to help parents make the right choices.

She gave a glance at the articles piled on the table. A college-lined notepad, new package of pens, and book with an unbroken spine. *Creating Stories Kids Will Love* had become a dust-gathering centerpiece. Her thoughts returned to her earlier encounter with Molly. "Old people are supposed to be responsible, like you." With a sigh, Nora figured perhaps she would start some reading or writing over the weekend.

She turned on the television with the remote and pushed a few buttons to find a channel that played continuous nature and wildlife shows. The documentary playing was about Alaskan polar bears. She liked that type of programming as it kept her mind entertained, but mostly occupied during off hours.

The Postponement Center, or TPC as most referred to the organization, had been Nora's life for the past seven years; ever since the postponement option had been legalized. Routinely she accepted extra shifts beyond what Dr. Thompson required. He didn't seem to mind paying the overtime and never complained when she labored through most of her vacation days.

After dropping out of college she became restless and disengaged from every job. She floated from employer to employer trying out all kinds of positions from an administrative assistant to retail cashier to theater ticket taker to a volunteer coordinator at a homeless shelter. At the finish of year two with TPC, Nora had exceeded her longest tenure with any of her previous occupations.

She stumbled upon the online listing by a private Austin based facility conducting a nationwide staffing search. She swore she would never return to her home state of Texas, but the opportunity sounded intriguing.

Postponement services had riled up some community groups. It had remained divisive and controversial from the start. That did not deter Nora. She interviewed well and they hired her despite her patchy work history.

The Client Liaison position seemed like the perfect fit and no one could say she didn't know all the ins and outs of the job after having been there for so long. Resigned that she never quite meshed in with many of her coworkers, she did have an excellent reputation with most of the clients. They trusted her. Of course, in her line of work, not every customer would end up happy, but does that ever occur?

When the polar bear show ended, Nora placed the half-eaten supper on the coffee table and refilled her empty glass.

A few minutes before midnight, with her sleep-inducing beverage long finished, Nora's head rested on the back of the sofa, a faint snore emitting from her gaping mouth.

The mutt looked up at Nora then hopped to the floor and began lapping up the remaining spaghetti from the china. The silver screen still flickered as the broadcaster tendered an impassioned plea enticing the audience to stay tuned for an amazing special: *The Life of a Shrimp.*

As Belynda licked the last drop of red sauce, the most recent late night commercial for TPC aired:

An upbeat female voice spoke over images of diverse women and couples beaming with expressions of satisfaction and fulfillment.

"Succeed," began the narration. A confident woman was shown leading a business meeting. Another shaking hands with a man as they stood in a huge corporate lobby.

The narrator goes on, "Discover." A smiling man and woman maneuvered a sail boat. Two women hiked a flower-filled mountain trail.

"Educate." Another woman listened to a professor in a classroom, then threw a graduation mortarboard in the air.

A group of twenty-somethings laughed and clinked their glasses together. "Enjoy," claimed the voice over. A couple danced in a crowded night club.

"Acquire." A woman received the keys to a new Mercedes. A man slid a two-and-a-half carat diamond engagement ring on a woman's finger. Then he carries her over the threshold into a beautiful new home, her hand-sequined wedding gown flowing.

A father observed while a newborn baby was laid in the arms of a mother. "Love," said the narrator in a softer tone and the background music tinkled with high piano notes. "Only you know when the time is right to bring a child into your life."

The advertisement offered contact information as the narration continued. "The Postponement Center. Find us at ThePostponementCenter.com or call 512-555-BABY (2229). Our professional and caring specialists are available twenty-four hours a day, seven days a week to answer your questions and schedule your confidential consultation."

The new mother on the ad kissed the forehead of her infant. "Because your life is for living," concluded the voice. Superimposed over the joyous happy new family were the company logo and slogan,

The Postponement Center - When the time is right.

A loud pounding caused Belynda to start barking and run across the room. Nora jolted awake, her heart throbbing. She wiped the corner of her mouth where the drool had pooled. Walking to the entry way, she confirmed her suspicion via the peep hole, and swung open the front door.

Belynda sprung into the neighbor's arms squirming with excitement. He stepped inside while turning his face away from the ecstatic wet tongue. "Okay girl, okay. I'm happy to see you too."

Nora yawned. "How was the visit?"

"Great. Sorry it's so late. The flight out of Chicago was delayed, then they lost my luggage," he said.

Waving a hand in dismissal, Nora picked up a box filled with dog toys, food, treats and bowls. "That's alright. We kept busy. Went for some walks..." She spied crimson-colored speckles on Belynda's chin hairs and glanced back at the coffee table. The dinner plate sparkled like it had come straight from the sanitation cycle of the dishwasher. Nora gave Belynda's ear a gentle tug, "...Shared a few meals."

"Why don't you get a dog, Nora? You're so good with Belynda," her neighbor said.

"Nah, I'm not home enough. I never know what my schedule's going to be —."

"Doggy day care," he asserted. She shook her head. "Dogs make wonderful companions," he pressed. Nora handed him the box of goodies and edged him towards the door recalling when once on a whim she adopted a stray basset hound.

Falling asleep that first night with the animal at her feet had felt right. At 4:45 a.m., instead of a rooster, she awoke to howling and once able to get her eyes focused was appalled to find everything within reach chewed: her cell phone, the legs of her bedroom chair, training materials from the job she was scheduled to start in two days and the electrical cords to the lamps by the bed.

"I don't like getting attached," said Nora trying not to think about the weeks of guilt she bore after returning the dog to the pound less than sixteen hours after bringing him home.

"You would have fun with a pet," the neighbor went on blinded to Nora's clear body language cues. He began grating on her nerves. "Maybe a cat? A gerbil? A para —"

"I'd rather have fun getting some sleep," Nora cut him off, happy to bolt the door behind him. She switched off the light and headed to bed. The dishes could wait until morning.

CHAPTER 5

Nora pushed through the sky blue curtains to find a young woman lying in a hospital bed. Her face was rosy and swollen, and her stomach was enormous against such a small frame. A woman sat beside her in a padded chair. "Good morning, Jennifer," Nora said with a slight smile.
"Hi Ms. Collins. This is my mom, Brenda."
The mother reached out her hand, but Nora ignored the handshake offered and opted for, "Good to meet you." She held out the tablet to Jennifer and handed her the stylus. "Just need one last signature here."
After resting her head on the pillow, Brenda brushed her daughter's forehead. "Jen's really nervous," the mother said with a worried expression.
"No, I'm not, Mom," protested the daughter, embarrassed by her mother's doting.
Nora gripped tight to the clipboard and promised the eighteen-year-old that it was very normal. "Tim couldn't make it?"
Jennifer released a long disheartened sigh and shook her head in disappointment. "He had some exams this week. I tried to get him to reschedule but he said we wouldn't be able to see the baby anyway, so no big deal."
Brenda looked down and tugged on the bottom of her shirt keeping a grimace from her daughter. Nora never had been

introduced to Tim. Another Client Liaison met with the couple a few months earlier when they came to sign paperwork authorizing the procedure.

Jennifer exhibited such an eagerness to understand everything about the process. "My friend told me to watch an old movie *Encino Man* where the caveman is frozen in this humongous block of —"

"Yes, I saw the film," Nora assured her client, who at the time was a senior in high school. "Postponement technology is much more serious than a silly adolescent story."

Jennifer laughed. "Well yeah, I figured," she said with a playful sarcasm realizing her Liaison didn't have much of a sense of humor.

Nora had been both impressed and envious with how Jennifer researched and weighed all her options, scheduling several meetings before making an intelligent conclusion. It was immaterial to Jennifer that she held her parents' emotional support and access to their wealth. Nora wished she had been more discerning during her own young adult life.

A nurse parted the draperies and announced, "Time to head back now." Jennifer received a sufficient apportion of hugs and kisses from her mother before Nora pointed Brenda on her way to the waiting area.

Pretending to conduct important business on her tablet, Nora kept an eye on Jennifer being wheeled down the hallway. The nurse turned a corner then punched a wall plate causing two sets of double doors to open allowing her to move the gurney through the entry and into the operating room.

Nora followed a little ways back looking at her watch. There was still time before her next appointment, so she could hang out for a while longer. She slipped through the first set of doors and peeked through a window on a second door. It gave a perfect view into the sterile white room and all that transpired.

Inside were Dr. Thompson, an anesthesiologist, two surgical nurses and a neonatologist specializing in cryonics. As everyone busied themselves with stainless steel instruments and medical equipment, the anesthesiologist spoke in a pleasant and calming manner to his patient. Nora heard only muffled words, but she knew the routine by heart.

"You'll be completely sedated during the entire operation," he explained. "You should not feel any pain." Of course, she asked more than most patients, but he took the time to answer all her inquiries.

Nora checked to make sure no one had noticed her standing there and she glanced at the time again. "Come on, Jennifer, quit asking so many questions," she mumbled to herself tapping her foot.

Once Jennifer seemed satisfied, he covered her nose and mouth with a mask. "Alright, go ahead and count backwards from one hundred."

The countdown began. Even though her voice was inaudible, in most cases it only took to ninety-seven to put the person under. The anesthesiologist viewed various monitors before nodding at Dr. Thompson, "Mother's down."

Nora stepped away from the windows upon hearing voices and the sound of a wheelchair moving down the hall. Despite being caught and reprimanded before, she couldn't resist the temptation once in a while and peered back through the window.

One of the nurses passed a long, slender syringe to Dr. Thompson who located it low on Jennifer's abdomen. His eyes remained affixed on a high-powered ultrasonic video image guiding the needle's insertion into the hip of the fetus. Once placed, the doctor delivered anesthetic at a slow, steady rate. The

23

anesthesiologist scrutinized levels on another device, before calling out, "Neonate's ready."

Using multiple types of blades, scissors and clamps, along with a slew of apparatus only surgery staff would understand, Dr. Thompson performed a traditional cesarean section. Nurses dabbed and suctioned up blood from the seven-inch long incision made about five inches below Jennifer's belly button. Three minutes later, he extracted the slumbering baby girl.

Nora stifled the tiny gasp of amazement that occurred each time she watched the miracle of birth. She was late for her meeting but they could wait a little longer.

While Jennifer was sutured back up, the two nurses moved swiftly to clean up the newborn and administer a basic examination taking measurements, swabbing the inside of her cheek and conducting a blood draw. The girl was laid into an open crypod unit positioned on top of a cart.

The neonatologist began her work. Injecting into the thigh of the infant, she administered a precise dose of cryo-protectant solution. Massaging the baby's extremities hastened the drug to circulate throughout the blood vessels protecting cells by preventing the formation of ice during cryo-preservation.

The specialist closed the lid of the crypod and entered keystrokes on the keypad. Five seconds later the unit filled with a swirling white mist rapidly cooling the baby's body temperature to negative 196 degrees Celsius in a matter of moments. The blue light popped on indicating the successful postponement.

Nora almost dropped her tablet when her phone rang. Dr. Thompson heard the faint ring and looked towards the door but the spying Client Liaison had ducked away in time.

Ruben Martinez' name displayed on her screen. When she realized who it was, her heart skipped a beat. Those calls always meant a challenge. "Ruben," Nora answered.

CHAPTER 6

Nora slipped from the operating room doorway and hurried down the hall. The conversation held no niceties and proceeded straight to the point.

A mix of hope and frustration came through in Ruben Martinez' question, "Anything new?"

"Not yet," said Nora.

"You know it's getting harder."

Nora knew that to be true. She had been convincing Ruben and Sylvia Martinez for quite some time to hold off on reanimating their son, but it proved more difficult with each interaction. "Believe me, waiting is better."

He launched into his regular woes as a couple walked past Nora. She smiled at the newborn baby in the woman's arms.

Nora entered the spacious lobby. The grandiose glass block wall stood as the ultimate symbol of TPC's success. Cubes cast shifting hues of blue, yellow and pink depending on sunlight changes during the day. The room generated a warm and welcoming ambience for current and potential clientele.

The waiting area contained two dozen newly re-upholstered extra broad reception chairs, unblemished and lush banana plants and African ears, and the faint aroma of fresh brewed coffee. On the beveled-glass tables were a dizzying array of the latest *People*, *Life and Style*, *Sports Illustrated* and numerous parenting magazines.

Unable to listen to Ruben's repetitive concerns any longer, Nora interrupted him, "Sorry, Ruben. I'm late for an appointment; I have to go." She did not wait for his reply and disconnected the call. He would understand because Ruben was the utmost living definition of patience. His wife? Volumes of complication there.

Several people awaited their appointments. The online application she reviewed prior to the scheduled meeting offered insights. Nora had not met nor spoken to her next clients, yet she felt confident in her uncanny ability to read certain tell-tale signs after years of interactions.

Nora scanned the faces. "Where are you Mr. Andy and Mrs. Arlene?" she muttered preparing for her guessing game. She settled in on a close to thirties man sporting a classic red power-tie atop the traditional white button down shirt: *the right age range.*

A pregnant woman waddled her way back from the restroom. She wore a starched maternity business suit, exhibited a flawless hairstyle and perfect makeup, and carried a small handbag: *professionals facing a first pregnancy.*

Data submitted in advance indicated home ownership: *steady income and financially stable.*

Mother near due date: *motivated to make a decision soon.*

Things appeared likely for a sale and happy customers. Nora remained on track that month to make her highest bonus ever. Despite those demonstrators circulating out front, business kept increasing.

From her observations, Nora could also deduce with striking accuracy the health of a couple's relationship.

Andy pretended to read the local *Austin-American Statesman News*, although he failed to focus on any particular article: *he didn't want to be there.*

When Arlene returned from the bathroom and eased into the chair next to her husband, he had not bothered to look up or shown any concern: *he was resentful.*

Arlene picked up one of TPC's marketing brochures and devoured the information front to back then started re-reading it again: *she needed a postponement to work.*

The cover of the pamphlet displayed a prominent claim:

GOVERNMENT APPROVED CRYONICS IS ENDORSED BY LEADING OBSTETRICIANS AS A VIABLE AND SAFE CHOICE FOR PARENTS TO MAKE.

Here's my couple, Nora thought.

She walked to the caramel and chocolate colored marble counter. The receptionist, Christine, stood staring out the front doors to the edge of the property. Beside her was Kathy, a whiny individual with a peppery demeanor employed at TPC's Central facility. She held a recognizable interoffice manila envelope in her hand.

"Why don't they have something better to do?" mused Christine. Nora snuck up behind them.

Protesters surrounded a man and woman and began talking at them. The red-head motioned towards the building and waggled a scolding index finger at the couple.

Realizing Nora's presence, Christine scurried back to her desk while Kathy and Nora followed.

"Morning," Kathy said rather blasé.

"Good morning," Nora responded to her counterpart. There was no love lost between them. Most staff members of The Postponement Center had experienced Kathy's intense criticism at one time or another — Nora being no exception. At best Nora tolerated her. They both held the Client Liaison position, yet worked in different facilities. On occasion they covered for each other so things were better off kept cordial, albeit strained.

"Is that for me?" Nora said gesturing at the envelope.

Kathy exhaled and shoved it to Nora. "Yes. New gal in records missed the courier for the hundredth time. You'll need it for this afternoon. I'm not sure where they hire these people from. They certainly can't function in a professional place of employment..."

Nora exchanged a quick glance with Christine about Kathy's dramatics and transferred the envelope to her for handling.

Kathy dragged on, "They don't know how to show up to work on time or dress properly..."

Christine pointed at the Fuller's. Andy now flipping through a magazine; Arlene folding and shoving the brochure into her purse.

Kathy continued unaffected by the obvious disinterest in her rant by her coworkers. "...let alone answer the phones, file accurately, and handle clients —"

"Excuse me." Nora walked away glad to have a reason to escape. Kathy paused for three seconds before snapping her head back to Christine and going on.

Nora's guess had been right about the couple and she approached. "Mr. and Mrs. Fuller?" They raised their heads. "I'm Nora Collins. Please come on back." The trouble on the homefront grew palpable when Andy stood and moved in-step behind Nora, leaving his wife to struggle to her feet and lag behind.

CHAPTER 7

The couple followed Nora into a bright and welcoming mid-sized conference room with a round mahogany table and four chairs. A second, smaller but still striking, glass block wall provided a sound barrier and obscured privacy from the lobby. From a row of high windows, light streamed in adding a natural warmth to the buttery colored walls.

Strategically placed mini accent lights were positioned to feature several mounted pictures professionally captured and custom framed photographs of sweet innocent infants and cherub-faced toddlers.

A hint of jasmine infused the air. Today's fresh cut flowers, Siberian iris with graceful blue and lavender blooms arranged in a crystal vase set on a side table. Subdued piano notes played in the background barely audible, but present. The room was designed to bring tranquility to its occupants from all senses.

Andy perused the children's images. "Those are actual past clients," Nora said but received no response from him. "Would you like some water?" The couple accepted and she poured cool filtered liquid from a china pitcher filling two goblets. Arlene pulled her chair out far enough to accommodate her immense belly.

After Nora delivered the refreshment, she sat down herself. She widened her eyes, "Made it through the activity outside, I see." They nodded. "We apologize for the inconvenience."

Nora noticed the blank 'Referred By' box on the application. TPC's Marketing department drilled it into the Liaison's heads that they must obtain referral sources for tracking accurate statistics. "So how did you hear about The Postponement Center?"

"I saw your commercial," said Arlene.

Nora noted the appropriate spot. "Thank you for coming in. I'm a Client Liaison, your primary contact throughout the entire process from beginning to end: applications, scheduling, procedures, and maintenance."

"You've worked here awhile?" Andy asked.

"Since TPC opened," replied Nora.

"So you understand how everything works?"

When she first started in the position, she would get offended by people who seemed to question her knowledge of everything. Over time she grew used to it and expected it from those individuals who were more uncertain about the procedure. Those inquiries came in most instances from the men.

"I do." Nora's eyes fell to her tablet. "A computer software salesman and an assistant vice-president of public relations."

Arlene explained. "We moved to Austin a couple years ago. My company is neck deep in merger talks so my boss was not very happy when he found out I was expecting." She settled her hands on her bulging tummy. "You can see, I'm pretty far along and so we need to know if a postponement will work for us."

Nora nodded and filled in the form's next blank with a ONE while asking, "Your first pregnancy?"

Arlene took a sip of water then glanced at Andy who averted his eyes to the nearest photograph — a beautiful newborn with milky white skin and a pink bow affixed to a thick mop of jet black hair. "I've been pregnant twice before, but this is the first one I'm taking to term."

Nora did not look up nor flinch and replaced the ONE with a THREE. She guessed that wrong.

Andy hastened to add, "It's a girl." Nora began to recognize he was not onboard with this option yet.

"Congratulations. Why don't I explain about our services here," Nora carried on with a pleasant tone. She gave her tried and true twenty minute sales presentation using slides featuring glossies of smiling satisfied customers, diagrams of the crypod technology, and a flowchart of the various steps for the plan of action.

After hearing all their Client Liaison had to say, Andy leaned back in his chair. "What about when we want to bring our baby girl home?"

"Only you can determine the best time to bring your baby home. As long as your account is in good standing, you call us a few days ahead of time and we schedule the reanimation. In other words, we return your daughter to a conscious state."

"How long does it take?" asked Arlene.

Nora knew she had succeeded in winning over the mother. After having dealt with so many of them over the years, she could detect a gleam in their eyes communicating relief that a solution had finally been found. "About fifteen minutes."

Arlene shook her head. "That's honestly amazing."

"It is amazing," Nora agreed. Glancing at her watch, she thought about the ton of paperwork waiting on her desk and needed readying for another upcoming meeting. She attempted to wrap things up.

"According to your application questionnaire, you have already qualified as financially able to pay the initial surgery expense and the monthly cryonic maintenance fees. I just need to gather some medical information to ensure you and your daughter would be eligible candidates for our postponement services." Nora tapped on her electronic device to pull up a document. "Then you can read through the agreement and we can put things in motion."

"Well hang on a sec," Andy said not caring for being rushed. "Do all the babies make it?"

Knowing now her focus must turn to convincing the father, Nora spoke with confidence repeating the explanation she perfected over the years. "A small percentage do not survive the postponement. The numbers are similar to general newborn mortality rates. Everything is done to assure the safe keeping of our infants and we report to you any findings of concern."

Andy shifted in his seat. "What do you mean?"

"All decisions are made in advance as to what will happen in the unlikely case that there is a detected issue."

Andy and Arlene's eyes met for the first time. Arlene spoke, "Detected issue?"

Nora went on. "As with any birth, occasionally there are apparent visible concerns or defects. Parents simply choose if postponement would continue or be terminated should this rare and improbable situation occur."

"I read online about people postponing babies with problems," Arlene said.

"Postponing doesn't cause or eliminate these situations, the procedure merely puts them on hold until the child is reanimated," Nora kept her voice light. "This gives more time for the development of potential treatments or allows the family preparation time for bringing a special needs baby home."

Arlene frowned. "Why can't you decide about that later?" Andy shot his wife a scowl, like their decision would be any different.

Remaining unfazed, Nora continued. "For one thing, it is the law. Parents' wishes are determined beforehand so no matter what, the correct surgical course can be handled while both the mother and baby are still anesthetized. Sometimes people choose to release newborns with serious issues for adoption. We have a growing list of wonderful, loving people willing to embrace special needs children."

Andy shook his head, "We would never do that."

Nora sounded agreeable. *The Fuller's might not make the choice to give their baby up for adoption if she had a severe health complication.* "I understand. We just have to let you know all your options." But Nora witnessed such choices many times; parents who quietly signed away their unborn child should there be something wrong with him or her, planning to tell their friends they were waiting for some medical miracle.

Nora picked up her tablet hoping the couple would sense her need to finish up. "What other questions may I answer for you?"

CHAPTER 8

Across from Nora sat Carl Douglas., a short, borderline obese man in his late forties. Nerves triggered a twitch below his left eye and he fiddled with his watch. "Thanks for meeting with me."

"Sure. Christine said you have some questions?"

Carl rubbed his receding hairline with his fingers. "I'm in a weird predicament."

Nora knew there were no new situations. She had heard them all before. "Just go ahead and tell me what's going on, Mr. Douglas."

"Please, it's Carl." She nodded and waited for him to continue. He re-positioned himself in the chair, drank half a glass of water and did not make eye-contact at all. "There's this woman, her name is Leanna. I met her in a bar two years ago. I'm usually not one to attract women but —"

"Did you sleep with her, Carl?" Nora interrupted not needing nor wanting to be privy to all the intimate particulars.

He looked up. "Surprisingly, yes. Only once. I tried to track her down, but she never returned to the bar and she gave me a phony number. I didn't hear anything from her until three months ago. She must have found my phone number. Mine wasn't fake. She left me one message, but no way to call her back."

"You are a father."

Carl blinked his eyes. "Yeah, me, of all people. Leanna said I had a kid at The Postponement Center and if I wanted her, I should get in touch with you guys."

"You are certain the baby is yours?"

He shrugged, "I didn't believe it at first, just kind of figured it was a joke, especially because she never called me again. But when I finally told my father about her call, he told me to man-up and, if I did create a kid, I should do the right thing."

"She reached out to you ninety days ago?" Nora asked.

"It took me a while to figure out how I felt about the news. And you know what? I really want the little girl. Chances are slim that I'll have another chance to be a dad. My job is steady and pays decent and my parents said they would help me raise her." Carl smiled.

Nora typed on her tablet, "What was Leanna's last name?"

"Uh, Anderson or Henderson — yeah, Henderson. Leanna Henderson. I saw some mail in her apartment."

Scrolling through a list, Nora said, "Found her."

Carl's eyes grew large. "In her message she said she stopped paying, did she?"

"I can't release that information." She kept her tone calm, but the situation reflected direr than Carl could imagine and Nora leaned closer. "Her postponement was categorized as a single mother."

"Well, we definitely weren't together, but it does take two." Carl chuckled, but Nora did not.

"Let me explain how this works," said Nora. "The mother is legally obligated to exhaust all avenues to find the father. Once she proves she completed her due diligence she can still move forward with postponing, but she signs off and becomes solely financially responsible."

"She said she tried to find me?"

Nora squeezed her lips together, "I'm not supposed to say." Then she gave her head one nod.

"But, we talked about where I worked and she never contacted me," Carl said. "She must have had my number."

"This happens."

"Obviously, she didn't want to have anything to do with me."

Nora referred back to her tablet. "Since she stated she was single —"

Carl touched his chest. "Well, I'm here and telling you, I'm the father. What can I do?"

The technical explanation continued. "If a man comes claiming he is the rightful father, he must hire an attorney to file a claim for custody of the child. The process is often convoluted and can become lengthy. Sometimes a private investigator is also needed to try and find the mother.

He shook his head, "That's crazy."

"That is the law."

"Okay, how do I get started?"

"I will email you all the details on how to proceed, but you must act very quickly, Carl." Nora referenced the case notes. "Leanna stopped making payments close to one hundred and twenty days ago and collections cannot locate her. Preliminary proceedings for forced adoption are already underway."

CHAPTER 9

Nora was bent over Toby's crypod. "Morning little man," she whispered while running her hand along the top of the cool unit.

Amisha flew into the room making Nora bolt upright, "Oh, there you are. Christine's trying to find you. Your appointment's waiting."

"Thanks. Everything looks good in here," commented Nora, attempting to veil her real reason for being in Crypod Holding, again.

Amisha wiped her forehead and spoke aloud in an over-dramatic manner. "Oh great, I was so worried, Nora. Thank goodness you saved the day."

Nora didn't bite on her coworker's sarcasm and strode out of the room with the whoosh of the closing door behind her.

Nora introduced herself to her new clients as they sat around the mahogany table in the conference room. She perused the application on her tablet noticing a check mark in one particular box. "I see someone referred you to The Postponement Center. May I ask their name?"

Patricia Evans, seven months pregnant, sported a perpetual frown on her face evidenced by three deep lines between her tweezed-thin eyebrows. "Somebody at my work used you guys a few years ago."

"Wonderful, who was that? We like to recognize those individuals with a generous personal gift card should it turn into a postponement."

Shawna Evans, the other woman, mouthed, "Wow."

"Yes, it's quite generous," said Nora. She liked the program not only because it brought in more business, but because she was the one who suggested it to Dr. Thompson. He had been impressed with her initiative during those first few months.

"Lea or Lonnie or something," Patricia said, not caring to even remember.

"Lonnie McDermott?" Nora asked knowing that Lonnie and her husband frequently recommended couples to TPC.

Patricia rolled her eyes, "I don't know."

Shawna spoke up, "Yes, it was Lonnie. Patti's been getting forgetful lately." Patricia glared at her spouse. Shawna smiled and leaned back balancing her chair on the back two legs.

"So, we've a lot to do before we could ever raise a family," said Patricia, her focus now back on Nora.

"We're both out of town almost every week," Shawna chimed in.

"And we need a much bigger house," Patricia added.

Removing a pencil stuck behind her ear, Shawna scratched the middle of her back. "I should be a partner in my firm in the next three years. Then we might be able to handle kids."

Patricia's head snapped to Shawna. "I'm not sure. We don't want to begin until everything's settled."

Nora engaged a common sales technique by making an empathetic statement, although she had not been in their exact situation before. "Seems wise to prepare with the right size house and an appropriate financial position. Parents don't always consider these things when choosing to start a family. Of course, all those decisions depend on what's best for the both of you."

The couple nodded in agreement.

Shawna grinned and sat forward. "Patti and I have a strategy here." Nora cocked her head. "I'm planning a pregnancy for next year. We were going to try and go through it together, but —"

"That would have been impossible," Patricia blurted out.

Shawna gave a hearty laugh. "Yup, way too many hormones for one household." Nora offered a polite half-smile as Patricia rolled her eyes again and Shawna continued. "We figure since we can have healthier kids while we're young, why take the chance we can't later on for some reason."

Nora had heard this reasoning before. "Tucking a few away for the future."

"Exactly," Shawna agreed, leaning her chair back once again.

Patricia shifted in her seat, impatient about the meaningless chatter. "Is there any way I can do this early? I'm tired of looking so fat."

Nora stifled a chuckle and cleared her throat before answering the question. "Unfortunately not." Patricia's eyes rolled back in their sockets a third time as she let out a disappointed grunt.

CHAPTER 10

People roamed around the modern art gallery contemplating the array of artwork from emerging Austenite talent: still life in oils, landscapes in charcoal, chemical warfare in water colors.

The makeup of the two dozen visitors seemed as eclectic as the compositions balancing upon the easels. From the wealthy wearing flashy over-sized jewelry and carrying the most recent electronic gizmos in their hands to those in faded cut-offs and flowing tie dye chiffon, all were happy to wander around consuming free alcohol. People carried miniature waters, or plastic cups of crimson cabernet or rosy zinfandel provided by the curators.

Michael Collins drank a rich black homemade vintage. He hated the cheap generic wine served at these functions so he always finagled his way in with his own. "Sulfite allergies," he would inform the unsuspecting hosts.

Next to him sat two brown lunch sacks, one empty glass and two bottles of fermentation — one already uncorked. His work trousers bore various lines of poorly pressed creases and his shirt showed no evidence of an iron at all. His shoes were in serious need of a shine.

Michael's chiseled features became more prominent as he frowned at a particular canvas placed straight across from the oak bench. For sure the artist had been purposeful in placing the thin strokes and thick curves to depict, something. An obscure face? A rat's nest?

"Starting without me?" Nora cut in on his musing by appearing at her brother's side.

Michael stood and she hastened the obligatory awkward hug. "You look like shit," he said noticing deeper wrinkles around her eyes than the last time they had seen each other.

"Nice to see you, too," she said, smirking.

"You been sleeping?"

Nora shrugged as they sat and he filled her glass half way. She held it up to him. "So, how's it feel to be forty-six?"

"Effing old." They touched their glasses together in a toast.

After the first taste, she nodded her head. "Mmm, this is delicious." She noticed the bottle had no label. "What is it?"

"Blackberry Vino."

She swallowed again allowing the fruity flavor with a hint of sweetness to drench her tongue. "I like it. Where do you buy it?"

A grin spread on Michael's face, "There is only one source." She grew suspicious that he was up to something. "This buddy of mine from work makes all his own. He's got the whole set up in his basement."

They took another sip and stopped to observe a mother scold and drag her four-year-old outside by his arm. "Ouch," Michael said. "Anyhow, I have no clue how to do it, but I want a room to ferment some grapes, or better yet, brew beer. Too bad everyone else has the house full of so much crap. Oh, did I mention that this winemaker friend is a highly successful single guy?" He winked at his sister and she shook her head — she should have guessed. "Really, you should find yourself a man."

"Really, you should shut up."

But he didn't. "Join some single groups or sign up for one of those online dating —"

"Michael."

"They say fifty is the new thirty," he continued as she ingested more fruit of the vine. "How come we didn't meet for your big one?"

She ignored his comment. "How are the kids and Stacie, Suzie — what's her name?"

He sighed, "Bree. Like the cheese."

Nora thumped her forehead, "Right."

"Perhaps if you came around more often or called once in a while you'd —"

"I've been busy," she interrupted.

He raised a solo brow having heard it all before. He followed her gaze to the abstract masterpiece in front of them. "I know, I can't figure out what the hell it is," he chuckled and handed her one of the bags. "Turkey, pepper-jack, pickles, am I right?"

"Wow, impressive," stunned he remembered.

"I still have ninety-nine brain cells left."

As Nora unwrapped the sandwich, her mind wandered back to when, as kids, she and Michael would sit on their back porch drinking tart lemonade and eating grilled cheese on white bread. Their hours were consumed with counting and guessing games since they lived so close to the interstate. How many white vans would pass within five minutes? How many semi-trucks would turn off the highway? How many blasts of the horn would the freight train make on its route through town?

There were three community picnics during the summer months: Memorial Day, Independence Day and Labor Day. Parents sat under the park trees and bantered back and forth about political misgivings, the Vietnam War and the space program. The elementary kids busied themselves running around playing Kick the Can, Red Rover and Freeze Tag, while the teenagers found ways to ditch their younger siblings by discovering dark places in which to steal kisses from each other. The gatherings always ended with a huge bonfire lasting until exhausted parents dragged their reluctant children away.

Nora and Michael's father always stayed until everyone else had gone home. She adored that about her father. He had been a science teacher and a beloved assistant football coach at the small town high school. His "beautiful bride," as he often referred to Nora's mother, worked part time as a bookkeeper for the local city utility office. She made the best pickles and —

"Earth to Nora Bora," broadcasted Michael who was attempting to garner Nora's attention. "Hellooo."

One side of her mouth curled up hearing the nickname her brother called her as a kid. "Sorry. So you even got the pickles right, sweet not dill."

"Can't take credit for that," he said. "That goes to Bree. She's committed to making all the family meals, now. Trying to fit in, I guess."

"You going to marry her?"

He cocked his head, "Probably."

"What do your kids think?"

He exhaled, "They put up with her."

"How are the boys?"

Michael downed the remainder of his wine before answering. "They're driving me nuts. No matter how I try and steer them forward, they end up shifting into reverse."

"I'm sure it must be the age." A safe standard answer she figured.

"Yeah? From the start, they've been a pain in the ass. You were the one who wanted children, not me."

She sipped, taking in another painting across the room to feign her attention.

He mimicked her as a young girl. "You used to say, 'I'm gonna have four kids and two dogs.' You remember that?"

"We get what we deserve," she said, focusing on the flawless round shape and over-abundance of sugar, recognizing the crumbly oatmeal cookie had been store bought.

He contemplated before chuckling. "So, Bree got Mom and Dad a new home a couple of weeks ago," said Michael and Nora arched an eyebrow. He pulled out his cell, scanned through his pictures and held out the phone for her to see.

On a shelf next to a portrait of their parents, sat an unusual item. Two twelve-inch high oblong vases each five inches in diameter; one bright sky blue, the other cotton candy pink joined together by a four-inch rainbow-colored, heart shaped container.

Nora cringed, thinking it was rather hideous while Michael inserted his fingertip into his ear and wiggled it. "Well, isn't that unique. Uh, is it —" she ran out of words.

He pointed to the picture explaining. "Well, obviously Mom's in the pink side, Dad's in the blue and then there are ashes of both of them mixed in this heart thingie in the middle. I guess there's some woo-woo type symbolism like it represents their two souls intertwining as one during this lifetime and for all their future lives together."

Nora tilted her head as Michael stuffed his phone back into his pocket. "I know. She found it online at some website in China or something, got it delivered to her work, moved all the remains herself and surprised me with it for my birthday." His eyes expanded. "Like I said, she's trying — perhaps a little too hard."

"Bree didn't even know Mom and Dad," Nora said to Michael while discarding a piece of romaine that had escaped from between the bread slices and landed on her shoe. "Maybe they don't want to spend every life between now and eternity together. It was pretty apparent they didn't even like each other the last few years."

Michael shook his head. "That is not true."

"Yes, it was. Whenever I was there they were constantly bickering. I remember getting all over Dad to stop being so mean to Mom."

"That's what happens when you don't feel well, Nora. They both were sick."

"Still, I think —"

"You were there once a year at the most," he said. "I was there every day. And I can tell you they were in love every moment for thirty-seven years plus six more for the years they dated."

She stared at the ceiling while calculating in her head. "They started dating at fourteen? They always told us they were eighteen."

"You would have found out a lot more about them if you'd stuck around," Michael uttered, old resentment in his voice.

They sat in silence as they ate. The air laid heavy with the reality that besides sending money, she had not helped her brother deal with their elderly parents.

Nora examined a baggie containing greasy potato chips and dropped them back into the paper sack. "How's the job going?"

Michael's sarcastic humor returned and he faked an over enthusiastic voice, "Oh, mucho primo fabulous." She glanced at him with a half-smile. He never tried to hide the fact that he disliked his long-term accounting position. "Only twenty-one more years to go."

The second bottle was opened. Michael gulped, Nora tried not to. Despite the desire to push the little buzz she had going into a full-fledged mood changer, she must return to work.

People went on perusing the paintings. Michael gave all the same answers he always did to all the same questions Nora always asked every time she saw him.

"So we talked all about my boring ass job, what about you?" he asked.

"You still rebuilding old cars?" was Nora's response.

He laughed. "Yup. Looking to find a '64 Ford Mustang. Strip her down and put her back together."

"Huh," she grunted. "Sounds fun, not." She struggled to come up with another subject before —

"You been putting a lot of babies on ice these days?"

She grit her teeth having wanted to avoid talking about her job at all. With reluctance, she took the bait.

"The term is cryonically preserved," she corrected him.

"Oh right, sorry." He grimaced while sticking up his thumb and examining it. "Hey, been meaning to get over there to get this wart removed." He snickered.

Not amused, she wadded up her empty paper bag with a loud crunch turning some heads around. "That would be called cryotherapy."

"Just 'cuz it's legal doesn't make it moral," he said.

"Parents should be able to determine what's best for themselves and their family."

He scoffed, "You sound like a freaking commercial."

Nora stood her ground. "Look, I have to explain these things to people six, sometimes seven days a week. I'm sorry I don't have some flowery way to describe it."

Michael held up his palms towards her, "Whoa."

"Why do we have to argue about this every time?" she snapped.

"We're not arguing, we're discussing," he responded.

They drank in silence; at least until he could no longer hold back. "You've put things in a storage unit, before." She released an audible moan. "You think it's stuff you want. You pay rental fees for years making some SOB wealthy until some financial crisis comes along and you finally admit you actually don't want the shit you had in there anyway and quit paying."

Nora felt herself becoming more impatient. "Parents don't do that to their children."

Michael elevated his eyebrows. He attempted to top off Nora's glass, but she waved it away. With a shrug, he dumped the remaining liquid into his own, held it up extending his pinkie, and reverted to his high-pitched mocking voice. "Oooh, I don't want my baby now because I'm too preoccupied with my cruises and pedicure appointments and —"

"Think of the babies that are saved," she argued.

With a disgusted tone, he said, "Nora. The people who run these organizations don't give diddly squat about these kids and definitely neither do the parents who deep dip them."

She consulted her watch in a blatant and obvious manner. It was exhausting fighting a battle that never ended. "It isn't that people don't want their newborns, sometimes the timing isn't right. Most of the time things are just more complicated," she said.

"I wish you would find another job. You're wasting your time hanging out with these neonates or whatever you call them."

Nora sprung to her feet surprising Michael and the nearby gallery patrons. "They are children!"

They stared at each other for ten seconds before she picked up her purse. Her face flushed and her hands trembled. He had crossed the line.

"Wait, I'm just teasing, Sis. You know me, I like a damn good debate."

50

But the damage had been done. Nora refused to make eye-contact and spoke her final words in almost a whisper, "Thank Bree for my lunch."

As she walked away, Michael called out after her. "Sorry. Come on, Nora Bora. You didn't finish your — Call me?" He held his hand to the side of his head, his fingers mimicking holding a phone.

The surrounding people stared at the commotion then turned back to the art pieces on display, whispering. Michael's shoulders fell and he poured the rest of the blackberry tenderness from her glass into his own, not wanting to squander even a drop of the precious substance that enabled him to get through the balance of his work day. He savored it while frowning at the mystery painting. *What the hell was that?*

With only five minutes before her next meeting, Nora popped into Crypod Holding to re-center herself after her visit with Michael. Amisha was gone, giving Nora the freedom to greet many of the sleeping babies. Just being in their presence brought a calm and put a smile on her face. These were her children.

CHAPTER 11

Two attentive adults sat across from Nora in the conference room of The Postponement Center. Ben and Cassandra Mills gripped hands beneath the table and leaned forward in their chairs. Documents lay spread in front of them as Nora explained the different sections of the contract.

This mid-forties man and woman had just celebrated their eighteenth wedding anniversary and had been waiting for over four years to adopt. Now they topped the list for receiving the next infant going into TPC's adoption program.

"Will we find out anything about the mother and father?" asked Cassandra.

Nora shook her head, "We never know which baby it will be as the parents' decision to keep or give their child up isn't finalized until the postponement or reanimation actually occurs. Sometimes people change their mind."

"You mean they could take the baby back?" Cassandra said.

"Oh no," Nora reassured. "Once on the official listing, the biological parents forego all legal recourse. This means all adoptions are final."

The woman exhaled, relieved to hear that detail.

"We cannot reveal any specifics about their decisions. The only exception is if there are any health issues we are aware of with the newborn. We would explain those to you so you could determine if you wanted to proceed with adopting that special needs child or wait for another healthier one."

Ben and Cassandra glanced at each other. "We hadn't considered that possibility," said Cassandra.

Nora continued. "If the baby is discovered to have a critical physical or mental challenge later on we were unaware of, you still retain the option of letting the child go, but it proceeds as a private adoption. So you would remain responsible for paying for any expenses incurred until new adoptive parents can be found."

Recognizing the confused expression on her clients' faces, Nora clarified. "For example, one year down the road you find the infant suffered from a serious birth related problem and you decide you no longer wish to keep him or her. You are still financially obligated to care for the child until you can find new parents who wish to adopt."

"That has to be hard keeping a kid for a year only to give him or her up," commented Ben.

Nora offered her pat answer. "We don't get involved with parents' personal choices."

Using a pen, she pointed to another long paragraph on the stack of papers packed with difficult legalese words and phrases. "This refers to your willingness to absorb all overdue maintenance fees, should some exist. Also the costs associated with reanimation." The couple nodded in unison. "This payment is due in full within thirty business days of being notified that a baby is obtainable." She tapped a paragraph emphasizing the clause. "Should you be unable to meet this financial obligation by the end of those thirty days, the agreement is deemed null and void and your names are removed from the program."

"Absolutely, whatever it takes," said Ben, squeezing his wife's hand. "We've tried unsuccessfully for many years to have a child and we've endured the heart ache of several miscarriages. There is no way I would pass up this opportunity. I'm prepared to take out loans and borrow money to make this happen no matter what." He looked at Cassandra who bit her lip and brushed away an escaped salty drop.

Nora nodded and turned to the next page in silence. Ben refocused the conversation. "I'm curious. Are most of these babies available because people don't pay their bills?"

"Not necessarily. Sometimes parents simply alter plans for any number of individual reasons. They possess the right to put their postponed baby up for adoption at any time as long as fees are paid current and there is consensus between both mother and father."

She answered the rest of the Mills' questions attaining their initials on each section of the lengthy contract. Nora was anxious to wrap things up enabling as much extra time as possible before her next meeting.

CHAPTER 12

The warm breath on her skin, the weight of his head on her shoulder, the eventual cessation of his crying kept Nora cuddling and rocking the infant within her arms. "Shh, Thomas. Hush now," she whispered to the newly reanimated baby.

She stood outside the door of one of the exam rooms evading entry as long as possible. How could something so routine feel so wondrous, so tranquil. Her eyes closed.

JC's counterpart for daytime security coughed as he approached. Hearing the overt cue, Nora hastened to open her eyes hoping he had not noticed — although he had.

The mild mannered and soft spoken Irish immigrant Brady McKenna had long passed full retirement age. "Another one going home?" he asked with his heavy accent.

"The big day is finally here for Thomas," she said.

"Aw, gonna miss this one," he said and she tilted her head. "Oh you should see him. The life of the party, this one. Dancing and singing in Holding. I was thinking about teaching him and the other youngins how to play charades."

Rewarding Brady with the slightest of smiles caused him to give his own dentured grin and hearty chuckle. "You ought to smile more. You've got enough worry having to deal with all those pregnant ladies."

Nora nodded, "That's the truth."

"Heaven only knows how I had the wherewithal to keep my mouth shut during my better half's five pregnancies."

She gave him another rare smile. Brady was one of the few coworkers that Nora liked. They spotted Dr. Thompson heading down the hallway towards them.

"Alrighty, off to lunch. I nabbed a couple of the missus sprinkle cupcakes this morning. But don't tell the little ones, 'cuz I don't like to share. See you around, Miss Nora." Wiggling the infant's blanketed foot, he said, "Take care, Sir Thomas."

Nora entered the examination room. She remembered Tracy Levine from almost five years earlier when she had met with her and her husband to discuss a postponement. Recently married, both held respectable jobs, appeared well attired and seemed quite cheerful. Still, Nora had not cared for the father at all. Tracy trusted him to determine what made sense for the two of them. The man's control over his wife disconcerted Nora.

Now this thirty-two-year-old mother sat dressed in outdated worn clothing likely from a charity organization. Her leg kept bouncing in continuous motion. She chewed on her fingernails though they had been bitten well below the fingertips.

From a tight hold, Nora released Thomas to his mother. Tracy's mouth fell open as she took her baby in her grasp for the first time. Joy and amazement moistened her eyes and they glistened as she embraced her son tighter. "Were there any problems?"

A few key strokes brought a blackened computer monitor to life. "Everything was perfect." Nora picked up and compared a signed document to something on the screen. Something looked odd.

"Where is the baby's father, today, Tracy?"

The woman kept her head lowered refusing to make eye-contact. "Oh, he couldn't make it," she said, her tone falsely over-confident. "He's out of town on business. Your phone person told me to get his signature notarized and bring that in."

Moving only her eyes, Nora's stomach lurched as she saw paling yellow and purple bruises on the woman's jaw and arms.

Tracy snapped her head to Nora, her eyes communicating her familiarity with adversity. "Please, don't send anything else to my home." The women stared at each other for an extended moment before Tracy buried her face into the powdery blue blanket. There was no more discussion and ample time afforded her client to compose herself.

After escorting the new mother and her son to the lobby, Nora's phone vibrated indicating a voice mail from Ruben. She couldn't ignore his calls any longer. However, first she needed coffee and she headed for the break room. As she brewed a fresh pot, she retrieved and listened to the message. It was the same as all his other messages.

With many years and hundreds of appointments behind her, Nora learned to keep her opinions and judgments about people to herself. Despite what her brother Michael claimed about postponing, it was a workable choice for many and, as long as the procedure remained legal, she felt committed to promoting and educating people about the option. Her job was not to sway parents to make specific decisions about their lives and the lives of their children — though sometimes she did. Sylvia and Ruben Martinez exemplified a couple she continued to influence.

Nora took time to drink her afternoon cup of caffeine before dialing Ruben's number. His phone only rang once before answering with "Hold on."

He exited the back door of The Breakfast Bite Cafe and stood by the dumpster in the alley. The cocoa bean colored apron tied around his waist matched his short hair and distressed eyes.

An unassuming silver crucifix encircled his neck. "I'm here. What'd you find out?"

"She hasn't got back with me yet," Nora lied.

He sounded bothered. "My wife's getting really nervous."

"I know it's hard to wait, but —"

"And, she's scared to get pregnant again," he cut in.

"There isn't anything wrong with having another baby," Nora reassured him as Amisha came into the lunchroom and stopped in front of the vending machine. Clocks could be set on her 3:30 p.m. visit to obtain her daily chocolate fix; a living proof of a Snickers and Twix addiction.

Desperation filled Ruben's voice, "But, it might have the same —"

"Ruben. Just hang on. Let me check and I'll let you know soon, I promise." Silence. "Ruben?" he gave an audible sigh and hung up.

Snickers had come out on top that day and Amisha unwrapped the candy and bit off a pleasing chunk as she left. Nora dialed another number on her phone. "Hey, can I stop by tomorrow night? I need to talk with you — Yeah, I have the new address."

CHAPTER 13

The next morning, Nora arrived to work relieved to see the protesters had either slept in or decided to picket the Central TPC location or the state capitol building. Every year during the anniversary month when postponement services became a viable option, a flurry of activity and reignited controversy kicked up. Nora didn't think about why the annoying sign-carriers were missing from the landscape, she was just happy of their absence.

Before she opened the lobby door, Carl Douglas called out to her, "Nora?" Surprised, she saw him emerge from a damaged Lincoln Town car likely given to him by his parents a decade or two ago. He sported three days of growth on his chin and his eye twitch had not improved. Wisps of hair on end screaming for a wash and a comb.

"Carl, I tried to call you," she said. "You're running out of time. I told you to act quickly. This can be a long battle and you're already late to begin."

"Will you tell them I need more time? I can't afford to pay for the attorney and also the private investigator," said Carl. "But listen, I can start paying the crypod fees."

Nora shook her head. "That won't work."

"Why not?"

"Because technically you are a stranger. There's no legal proof you are the father."

He rubbed his forehead. "So, I'll do a DNA test."

"It all must go through the proper process," Nora said.

"There has to be something you can do. You're an employee here."

She chewed on her lower lip, glanced around and then pulled her wallet from her purse. After counting out some bills, she pushed two hundred dollars into his chest. "Here. Find the rest."

"But, this isn't near —"

"I'm sorry. There isn't anything I can do," Nora hurried through the front door leaving Carl in his despair. He shoved the cash into his jacket and went back to his car.

As she walked across the stone tiled entry, out of the corner of her eye, she noticed Dr. Thompson standing at the reception desk with Christine. He was eyeballing Nora. Not stopping, she hastened her pace into the hallway saying nothing. She hoped he hadn't seen her hand Carl the money. She had been caught doing that before and it was not pretty.

CHAPTER 14

Francine and Alec fussed over the contented newborn held in Francine's arms. She touched the strands of fine red hair on his head. All the usual oohs and aahs were bestowed.

Nora stood back observing the parents with their newest family addition and also cognizant of the four-year-old boy with bright orange hair standing next to her. The sibling. The big brother. The formidably suspicious one. His arms folded tight, a scowl across his brow and a downturned mouth — unconvinced this was such a good idea.

"Aren't you happy to have a new brother?" Nora asked him. He shrugged his shoulders and pushed his bottom lip out further.

Alec observed his first son, "You think he looks like you?" The older boy studied the baby's face, crinkled his nose, with a violent shake of his head and turned his body away. Although every few seconds his gaze returned to the tiny package his mother embraced.

Francine tilted her head and glanced at her husband. "They're identical. I told you."

Nora crouched down by the boy and he gazed at her with glassy eyes. He fought hard not to cry but his chin began to quiver. "You already spent nine months with your baby brother," she said in a tender voice. "You boys are going to be best friends."

After a moment of consideration, the boy's eyes shifted back to the infant. With a gentle nudge from Nora, he shuffled closer. Alec picked him up and set him in a chair. With care, Francine placed the newborn into the clumsy arms of his brother — his twin, yet four years apart.

"Hi," said the little boy. He smiled when this funny new person squeezed his stubby finger. Having a younger kid hanging around might not be so bad.

Nora could not fight off a small smile. She noticed Francine clenching her jaw and Alec looking away. Expecting both parents to be more elated, more thrilled, the moment felt awkward. The mother and father were too melancholy and gloomy.

"We do offer a referral program if you might know others that could utilize our services. And, please call if we can help you again in the future," Nora said.

The mother straightened hairs on her son's head, "That won't be possible."

Nora nodded and gathered up the signed paperwork, "Stopping here?"

"My husband's not well." Francine put a trembling hand to her mouth and lowered her face. Sensing something was wrong, Nora turned to the father.

He pushed back his own tears and wrapped his arms around his family. "Just want to spend time with both my children."

Wanting to offer some privacy, she said "I'll be outside when you're ready," and she exited the room to wait in the hall. The emotional and intimate moment she had witnessed took her back to when she first heard about her own father's terminal illness. She had refused to deal with the truth and only visited him once during his final three years. Then he died. Nora wondered if this new baby, or even his elder sibling would carry any memories of their father at all.

CHAPTER 15

Erin Wood led Nora into an over-sized, vaulted ceiling, upscale kitchen. Everything was spotless. Nothing extraneous left on the counters: no dirty dishes nor water spots in the sparkling sinks, not one crumb or scuff on the tiled floor. Only a sole shred of evidence disclosed itself on the polished stainless steel refrigerator door: tiny smudged handprints about two feet from the bottom.

"This is obviously the kitchen," said Erin at the end of the house tour.

"This place is gorgeous," Nora commented. "I'm sorry I haven't been able to come over since you moved in. What's it been, a couple months?"

"Seven." Erin put her arm around her friend's shoulder and gripped hard. Nora's eyes closed and she recoiled at the physical touch. Acknowledging the discomfort, Erin released her hold. "It's wonderful to see you."

Nora had conducted a postponement consultation several years earlier with Erin, a former client, now friend. Erin found herself in her early thirties, unmarried and uninterested in establishing and maintaining a relationship. She was well on her way into a budding career as a bio-medical scientist and chose to bear a child on her own. Finding an agreeable donor to obtain what she required was not difficult. "Funny how inclined a guy was to provide what I needed knowing he could be completely un-obligated from any potential outcome," Erin had joked with Nora upon their first encounter. "The man is perfectly fine signing off on all the paperwork allowing me to assume full custody and financial responsibility. He only had to pay for a few things."

"What were those?" Nora couldn't help but ask.

"The three dates we went on until I became pregnant," she said and laughed at how clever she had been.

"So he understood ahead of time?"

"Absolutely." Without a hint of apology in her voice she added, "Way less expensive and non-evasive than artificial insemination and a hell of a lot more fun."

Erin kept her daughter postponed for five years. During that time, she continued advancing towards a highly respected researcher who worked on discovering drugs and therapies to treat and heal serious diseases.

Walking to a shimmering machine, a button was pushed and the scent of strong coffee filled the kitchen. Nora sat on a stool at the massive island. "You're doing well for yourself."

"Your star success story," Erin said, then laughed and pulled a disinfectant wipe from under the sink and in an instant the fingerprint proof on the refrigerator vanished.

Nora always considered Erin to be the proverbial poster child for the postponement option. She would not forget how confident she had been at her initial meeting, sashaying into the conference room wearing a fancy lace maternity dress with an Isabella Oliver designer label. Diamond studded bangles dangling from her slender wrist.

Placing baby blue flowered china cups on the counter, Erin sat down and Nora asked, "Where is Kayla, tonight?"

"Getting spoiled by my sister. Being a single mom isn't always delightful."

"Of course not."

"I never regret having her," she mused while looking at a recent photograph of her daughter inside of a red heart frame setting nearby. "She is my life and when I come home at night defeated by failed trials or having to deal with unbending executives, there she is with a grin as bright as the sun. Kayla makes things all better even if for a few brief moments."

Nora acknowledged the sentiments with a nod and half smile aware of what it felt like to become so attached; she experienced the same whenever present with the babies at work.

Erin shifted in her seat. "Why don't you adopt a baby?"

"You know it is against company policy."

"It doesn't need to be from your organization, go to some other postponement place." Nora shook her head but Erin didn't stop. "You could afford some delinquent crypod fees and have a kid of your own."

"My hours are too sporadic and I'm past motherhood years, anyway."

"That is not true. Perhaps child-bearing years but definitely not motherhood, you would be perfect. Might be good for you," said Erin.

"I appreciate your concern and suggesting it...again," Nora said raising her eyebrows at Erin who batted her eyelashes playfully. "So, I wanted to talk to you about something."

Undeniable she was moving on from that topic, her friend relinquished. "Sure, what's going on?"

"Remember the couple I mentioned a while back that have the baby with spinal damage?"

"Yes. The one you named Toby?"

Nora nodded. "I know you have a friend doing some kind of research in that particular area."

"A colleague of mine. One of a team of bio-med guys working on birth defects affecting the spine."

"Are they getting any closer?"

Erin took a sip of coffee. "They've made some major headway over the past several months but FDA approval can take years. What's the hurry?"

Nora cast her eyes down to the remaining few drops in her cup. "The parents are becoming restless."

Standing, Erin went to fetch the pot. "Well, I recommend you convince them to hold off. The longer they wait, the better chance there will be improved treatments, God willing, maybe a cure."

Nora sighed as she accepted a steaming refill and for the next hour, she inquired more about the challenges of Erin's job. Not that the minutia of the subject matter screamed fascinating, but it allowed for the conversation to continue until a sufficient amount of time had passed and she could leave.

She rather liked Erin. It just grew into a struggle to relate to her achievements, although Nora did recognize accomplishments in her own work. Possibly Erin's intelligence was intimidating, but Nora believed she also was smart. Graduating at the top of her high school class, carrying a 3.9 GPA in university work and her acceptance into medical college, none of which would have happened if she was stupid. Perhaps Erin's confidence and ability to stay committed to her projects long term disheartened Nora.

To be honest, she was not sure at all why Erin tended to make her uncomfortable at times. Yet because she held a connection to scientific study, for Toby's sake Nora would persist in staying in contact with her.

Around nine o'clock, the women said goodbye while Nora climbed into her 2011 old Honda Civic, grounds for more frequent prodding by Michael. "For as much as you make, Sis, don't you think it would behoove you to buy something new?" he chided on more than one occasion.

The driver's side door squeaked and the crack across the windshield insisted on spreading. "It runs and is paid for," she argued.

Nora played a voice mail message back from her brother, amused she had just been thinking of him.

"I've left three messages," Michael said sounding exasperated. "Would you please call me back?"

She tossed the phone on the passenger seat where it began ringing. Recognizing the incoming number, she answered. "Molly?"

The girl didn't respond.

"Molly, Are you all right?"

"No, Ms. Collins. I gotta problem."

Nora pulled away from Erin's house, pressing the cell to her ear. "Is your mom with you? Are you hurt?"

"I'm pregnant."

CHAPTER 16

After Molly answered Nora's questions about being certain about the pregnancy, Nora had to ask, "Molly, was this planned?"

"You mean like what my mom did with me?" Nora did not have any desire to delve into that backstory. "No. A stupid mistake, like most things in my life."

Speeding up, Nora merged on the still busy freeway. "How far along do you think you are?"

"At least three months."

"And you know who the father is?"

"Really? I'm pregnant, not slutty, Ms. Collins."

"I didn't mean to imply —"

"Of course, I do. It's my boyfriend. My mom says I should get an abortion. She said she's had them before," she sighed. "I'm not sure. It seems kind of mean not giving the kid a chance. Is that freezing thing you do super expensive?"

Nora knew Molly was trying to figure out life herself, little chance of being responsible enough to raise a child. She thought about how her parents might have reacted if she had become pregnant in high school. *They'd probably disowned me — well, no, not true.* "Postponing is expensive."

"So, just for rich people, then," mocked Molly.

Although many of TPC clientele were wealthy, not all fit that description. "There is something — a program you could check into," Nora said.

"Yeah, what?"

"A program designed to help parents gain access to postponement services. I can give you a card when I come home. But, you and the father must agree to some things."

"Is it like some kind of government program or something? My mom's been on those for like forever." Nora did not comment on Molly's observation.

"It is a non-profit organization designed to help," Nora said. "It would be best if you and the father met with them. They can explain how everything works."

Molly's sigh was audible. "My mom hates the father."

"Will you call them?" asked Nora.

After ten seconds, Molly responded, "I guess."

CHAPTER 17

Nora stood outside of The Breakfast Café. The old building had been given a facelift when the new owners had taken over the space. A sign in the window boasted the first brick and mortar location after humble beginning roots as a food truck.

Breakfast was their busiest and only meal of the day. From 4:00 a.m. to 11:30 a.m., the eating establishment guaranteed nonstop patrons. The challenge of finding parking confirmed the popularity of the restaurant.

The Austin food critics had awarded the cafe their highest rating for use of grass-fed locally sourced meats, organic produce, coconut oil and gluten-free alternatives. Nora thought the fare might be tasty, but she was not there to eat.

From her purse, she removed her phone and stared at the number for TPC. She didn't like telling blatant lies, but it happened when she believed her actions were warranted and worth the risk of getting caught.

Not long after Nora began with TPC, Dr. Thompson had pulled her into his office for the first of many times. "Nora, I recognize you are still becoming used to your new job and you are doing very well. Thank you," he said. "However, I do have a concern about your involvement with Nile and Elizabeth Lassen."

Christine had notified Nora of an unscheduled client who demanded to talk with someone with authority and refused to explain why. It was a busy day right before a national holiday and a three day weekend. Still new in her job, Nora wondered why this could not be handled over the phone, via email or at least waited until next week. She was directed to a woman pacing in the lobby.

"Elizabeth? I'm Nora Collins, how can I help you today?"

"Who are you?"

"I'm a Client Liaison."

Unfolding a paper, Elizabeth thrust it at Nora who accepted and opened it. She had seen the form letter in one of her recent online training courses.

"This is a collections issue. Christine can call to see if they can talk with you." Behind in her over-scheduled morning appointments, Nora started moving towards Christine's desk but Elizabeth grabbed her arm.

"No, please. I've tried to work with them." She took the paper back from Nora and pointed at one paragraph. "Listen to this. If all delinquent funds are not delivered to this office by Monday at 8:00 a.m., we will have no other choice but to take further action. That's in five days. What does that mean?"

Nora ushered the woman away from the lobby to a quieter area. She kept her voice low. "You are several months behind on your crypod maintenance fees."

"You think I don't realize that?" she blurted out. "I'm working two jobs and my niece is living with me. And, now my mother needs to move in because, well it doesn't matter. I don't know what they expect."

Nora knew what "they" expected and what would happen if she did not pay. "If you hit one hundred and twenty days, things reach an extremely critical state. What about your husband? Is he working, too?"

Elizabeth crammed the letter into her pocket. "Nile divorced me in March. I wanted to take full custody of our daughter and reanimate her but I can't because of your crappy policy."

Nora shook her head. "Changes like that can only occur if the account is current and parents agree. So you are both still financially responsible married or not. Is he helping at all?"

"Right," she said, her tone cynical. "He refuses to pay for shit. I'm the one getting all the phone calls from your people. My credit cards are maxed out and he doesn't care what happens to our child. I even considered filing bankruptcy, but you guys have that covered too."

Nora vehemently disagreed with some of TPC's policies and bankruptcy was one of them. Fees could not be discharged unless parents agreed to release their neonate for immediate adoption.

"And guess what else?" Elizabeth continued. "Now he's demanding I give him ten thousand dollars for custody. Who does that?" Her voice broke as Nora stared at her in disbelief.

She felt for the woman, but what could she do? The rules were the rules and she didn't make them. Christine walked by and Nora waved indicating the situation was under control.

"I told your phone people about everything, but they don't listen to —"

"We can't become involved with domestic disputes."

Elizabeth tried to stave off a full meltdown. "Please, Ms. Collins, can't you help me?"

Over the holiday, Nora found herself standing in the exterior hall in front of the apartment of Elizabeth's ex-husband. A strung-out, vagrant man sat on the ground nearby staring at her with steely grey eyes.

She knocked four times before a loud voice projected from inside. "Answer the damn door, Jasmine."

A woman looking way too tired for being in her early twenties, cracked the door three inches. Her greeting curt. "Yeah?"

"I'd like to speak with Nile Lassen. Is he here?"

"Who wants to know?"

"I'm Nora Collins from The Postponement Center."

The woman frowned as another yell came from behind her. "Who the hell is it?"

She left the door ajar and walked away. "Some old lady for you."

Nora's heart beat faster as she heard Nile stomp across the floor. He flung the door open and stood in bare feet and dirty jeans — no shirt. Visible needle tracks on his forearms. *No wonder he needed money.*

"What do you want?" he said in a gruff manner.

"Nile Lassen?"

He crossed his arms across his chest. "Who's asking?"

She handed him her business card. "I'm Nora Collins from The Postponement Center where your daughter is located." He raised an eyebrow and started to shut the door, but she stopped it. "No, please. I just want to talk with you a moment."

He leaned against the door frame. "Make it quick. I've got things to do."

Nora did not hesitate. "Elizabeth wants custody of your child." He shook his head sharply. "She's been trying to keep up with the monthly expenses, but, has fallen behind."

"If she wants the kid so much, she'll gimme what I want."

Not believing she was standing there arguing with no doubt a drug user if not a dealer that towered at least a foot and a half taller than her. She somehow found the courage to hold her ground. "You act like your daughter's some kind of commodity."

The man sitting ten feet away grunted and turned away.

"If these payments are not brought up to date soon, then —"

"Then what?" Nile said.

"Neither you nor Elizabeth retain anymore rights to your baby. The state determines her outcome. And, you won't get your money anyway."

Nile put his hand back on the door. "Are you done?"

"You just need to come to our office and sign one paper. Just one. Please, for the sake of your child. Come this week."

With a blank expression on his face, he slammed the door closed. The man sitting close by coughed and grinned up at Nora. "Hey lady. What you got for me?" She slipped away as she heard Nile and Jasmine begin arguing.

A few days later, Nora was called to the front desk and when she came, she was surprised to see Nile standing there with his hands shoved in his pockets. Without a word, she led him into the legal department where he signed custody of his daughter over to his ex-wife. Elizabeth was able to borrow enough money from compassionate friends to catch up the overdue crypod expenses and enable the reanimation of her baby girl.

"I saved a horrible thing from happening," Nora had protested to her new boss.

"Yes, I recognize that and although I appreciate your intentions, there is liability in the actions," said Dr. Thompson. "Proper procedures were made clear in your new hire orientation and they are in place for good reason. We have an obligation to protect our organization. Remember, the government has regulations prohibiting us from trying to influence the decisions of parents. So going to their homes or seeing them in any way outside TPC is against policy. I'm sure you understand it is to fend off lawsuits and safeguard not only the company but you, as our employee, as well."

Nora nodded even though she still felt justified in her behavior.

"I'm going to skip the write up this first time," Dr. Thompson said. "But you must follow protocol and not meet with any clients away from the TPC campus."

Nora exhaled as she readied herself to break policy for the nth time and lie about it to her employer. She dialed the number for her office. "It's Nora. I forgot about this doctor's appointment this morning and there's a long wait. So, I'm going to be late."

After hanging up, she opened the sparkling clean door of the Breakfast Bite Café.

CHAPTER 18

When Nora entered the Breakfast Bite Cafe, the smell of cooked pork and strong coffee struck her. Most of the seats were full of guests conversing and consuming their morning sustenance. A family of seven waited for their table to be set up. Mom and dad propped themselves against the wall, looking exhausted like they couldn't recall their last entire night's sleep. Twin babies sat in a dual stroller, one slumbering and the other squirming to break free from the straps. Two elementary-aged children shared a portable screen playing a Toy Story movie. A pre-pubescent boy or girl, Nora couldn't tell which, curled up at the end of the bench absorbed by an iPhone and earbuds.

She scanned the busy restaurant hoping to spot Ruben Martinez, but he was nowhere in sight.

Fresh cracked eggs splattered to a hot griddle and sizzled along strips of fatty bacon. Cooks, waiters, dishwashers and bus people scurried around the medium-sized kitchen engaged in their assigned duties.

Ruben Martinez pushed through the swinging door carrying a plate with a partially eaten omelet. Speaking in a low voice, he handed it to a perspiring man wielding a spatula for the taming of pancakes, hash browns and sausage. "Dice que esta muy picante."

The cook frowned, dumped the food into the nearby trash barrel and started to recook.

Heather, the manager, witnessed the interaction and strode over to Ruben. "We speak English here," she said, her tone brimming with ridicule. He lowered his head staring at the yellowed linoleum floor. "If you communicate properly, your orders will be right."

The other kitchen workers turned away, rolling their eyes. There was a not-so-secret joke that most of the employees wished their condescending leader would meander into the deep freeze and not return. Hearing a pause in the dirt being hurled, Ruben turned and walked to a small freezer. Inside he snagged a treat, then exited through the kitchen.

The dining room buzzed with customers ordering, devouring, and guzzling down mugs of coffee and expresso designed to power them through their upcoming day.

He liked working here, except for his manager. The food was always delicious, the coworkers were friendly, and the tips were excellent which contributed enough additional cash flow needed to pay the monthly TPC maintenance fee. In the afternoons and early evenings, he worked in a corporate office processing the company's packages and mail.

Moving towards the breakfast counter, he waved the ice-cream cookie in front of a man engulfed in a volume of classic science fiction short stories. Capturing his attention, the man smiled in acknowledgement and Ruben squatted down beneath the swiveling stools.

On the floor sat a five-year-old boy — his head buried in a book with animated pictures of lions and zebras. His eyes grew upon seeing the frozen dessert and he licked his lips when accepting it.

Nora approached the young hostess who was wiping something sticky off a menu.

"Good morning," she sang, way too chipper at such an hour. She couldn't have been more than sixteen but had a twelve thousand dollar smile with blinding white teeth.

"Morning," responded Nora. "I was looking to talk with Ruben Martinez."

"Sure, hang on." She beamed and waltzed to a table where Ruben was taking an order. After delivering the message, he glanced over to Nora, excused himself and walked straight to her, his brow furrowed. "Is my son, alright?"

"Yes, he's fine."

His eyes focused behind her as Heather showed up. "Are we eating or gabbing?"

"Uh...eating. Yes, eating," Nora said, not wanting to stir up trouble for her client.

"All right, then," the woman-in-charge said and snapped her fingers at the hostess. "Put her in two."

Nora followed the young woman to a small booth in the farthest back corner of the restaurant — the complete opposite side of Ruben's serving section.

Thirty minutes and three cups of caffeine later, Ruben slid into the seat across from Nora. "Your boss must be a joy to work for," she said, sarcasm emerging.

"It's a paycheck." His face remained serious.

She nodded in agreement; *that, it was.* "I talked about Toby with my friend that works in medical research."

He cocked his head, "Toby?"

Oops. Nora took care and didn't slip often with the names she bestowed upon the little ones sleeping in Crypod Holding. "Sorry. It is just what I call him."

She watched his shoulders drop and eyes wander upwards. "Toby. Toby Martinez. I like it."

Nora leaned forward, urgency in her voice, "Ruben, you must wait a while longer."

"My wife, she —"

"Having a child with special needs can be expensive and challenging," she interrupted.

He intertwined his fingers and compressed them. "We can do it. I'm working extra hours and putting money away and Sylvia got a raise last month and got promoted to a lead in the call center."

"That's all great, but the longer you can delay, the better." Ruben noticed his boss eyeballing them. "The better for Toby," clarified Nora.

He stood and looked back at her — a plea for help emanating from his brown eyes. "Can you talk to her?"

She hesitated but gave an eventual nod because she would do anything to prevent Toby from being reanimated until a cure was found. Sylvia wasn't the easiest person to deal with, but convincing her to continue waiting to bring her son home was Nora's only option.

Ruben walked away unable to avoid passing by Heather who launched into a badgering rant as she trailed him into the kitchen. Nora hurried out. She was beyond late for work.

CHAPTER 19

Nora crammed her purse into her desk drawer, picked up the tablet then turned smack into the chest of Dr. Thompson. He wore surgery scrubs and looked down at her. "Nice of you to come in this morning."

She stammered, "So sorry. Got held up at the vets."

Dr. Thompson placed his hands in his pockets. "This is your client and you know I don't like making them wait."

She moved past him and rushed out hoping this would not come back in another performance write-up. Passing through the fabric curtains, Nora found her patient sitting in the bed wearing a hospital gown and blue non-slip booties. "Hi," said Arlene.

"How do you feel?"

"A little nervous, actually."

Nora handed her the stylus and pointed on the digital form where to pen her final authorization. "Very normal. Nothing to worry about. Dr. Thompson is an experienced obstecryogenist and has performed hundreds of these surgeries. He is excellent. Just try to relax and you'll be finished before you know it." Arlene half smiled. "I'll keep Andy posted on your progress."

"I'd appreciate that. He's been grumpy all week. I hope he gets past all his childish behavior when this is all done."

Nora nodded, "I'll see you afterwards."

Arlene gave the tablet back and the Client Liaison left.

Fifteen minutes later, Nora stood in the corner of an examination room full of mischievous little people and one bossy mother. A toddler in a soiled diaper kneeled on the floor fascinated by the repeated opening and closing of one of the lower cabinet doors.

Gina, an unhealthy skinny woman in her early thirties, scribbled information on the paperwork. Four children, all under the age of seven, grew louder, fidgeting and fussing. "Shut up!" yelled the mother.

A six-year-old girl precariously held reanimated Stephany in her arms as Nora resisted the urge to help. Another child reached for a metal tray of pens and papers on the counter causing everything to clatter down. Gina jumped. With frazzled nerves, she slapped the child's hand, "I said don't touch anything. Pick that stuff up."

Nora did her best to keep her horror in check. "Looks like you've got your hands full."

"Your monthly fees are too damn high and my husband wants another tax deduction." Gina swiped a brochure entitled, Postponement Procedures, from a kid's hand. "He refuses to pay for it anymore. It was from a boyfriend anyway."

"She," Nora said.

Two of the children erupted into an argument resulting in a high-pitched screech from one of them. The flustered mother grasped the chin of the screaming child making his eyes expand in fear. "I...said...stop." As he cowered behind a chair, she snapped her head towards Nora. "What'd you say?"

"Not *it*, she."

The mother grabbed the shoulder of the little girl holding Stephany and yanked her as she spoke. "Well, THIS *she* is going to take care of THAT *she* because I don't have time."

TPC rules prevented employees from outward criticism of the decisions parents made about their neonates. The slogan touted everywhere on business letter head, in email signatures, on all marketing materials and even on the sign in front of the building, claimed, "When the Time is Right." This communicated that the adults had the right to choose when to bring their baby home and, unfortunately in this case, into whatever family dynamics existed.

"Perhaps you should consider adoption," Nora said.

At the end of what little semblance of patience the mother may have started with, Gina shoved the signed documents into Nora's chest. "Did I *ask* for your opinion?" Then she pushed and pulled all the children out through the door and herded them down the hallway. "Hurry up, come on!"

Nora gritted her teeth. Never having felt unwanted when she was a child, she could only imagine how this little one's life would unfold. "Goodbye, sweet Stephany," she muttered as the family disappeared into the lobby.

CHAPTER 20

A slow-walking bubbly woman with thick support-hose and boxy flat shoes approached Molly and her boyfriend as they sat in the TPC lobby. With a tired sigh, Betty plopped into a chair, smiled and patted Molly's hand. "Hello there, my dear. My name is Betty."

"Hey," managed Molly. "This is David."

"A pleasure meeting you, young man," said Betty with a pleasant tone having long developed the skill of masking private reactions to how the younger generation appeared these days. The sixteen-year-old slumped in the chair tugging at his scraggly attempt at a beard.

The elderly woman remembered when men wouldn't be caught dead with anything pierced through their ears, and nowadays this gauging thing made no sense. She also didn't understand the meaning behind the tattoos covering his arms — snakes and skulls and odd-shaped letters. Why on earth any man, let alone woman, would have more than a single anchor tattooed on his bicep was beyond comprehension. Yet, Betty loved volunteering to help these children, as she regarded them, ensuring they made the correct decision — the one she maintained to be best in these situations.

David grunted and picked at an inflamed red pimple on the back of his neck. "Need a tissue?" Betty said with a grin. He shook his head and wiped his fingers on his skinny jeans. The woman pushed down on her thighs to rise, "This way then." The young couple followed her down the hall.

Nora rounded the corner. "Molly."

"Hi-ya Ms. Collins." The girl stopped as Betty continued walking. She pointed to the boy behind her. "That's David." He offered a split-second glance in return.

"Betty will explain everything to the both of you," said Nora.

"K," responded Molly, then she leaned over and whispered in Nora's ear. "She smells like menthol cough drops and sticky hairspray. She's so archaic and crusty." Nora smiled slightly as the teens obeyed Betty's open hand motioning them into the conference room.

The volunteer winked at Nora. "They'll be fine," she mouthed as she entered herself and closed the door.

The three of them sat around the table. The girl slouched in her chair; the boy gazed at the happy kid pictures while incessantly tapping a pen on his knee.

"How far along are you, dearie?" the old woman asked.

"Four months."

Betty cocked her head. "You're awfully little."

"Yeah, but I'll probably get huge like my sister when she had her baby."

Betty studied her paperwork. "I'm happy you are both here. Often that is not the case." She bent towards David and he stared at her with no expression. "You are the father, aren't you?"

He shrugged. "Well, we only hooked up a few —" Molly jammed her elbow into his arm. "I guess," David added.

"Both mother and father must agree on the postponement. Since the two of you will be under eighteen when the baby is born, you'll each need to have a parent sign too."

Betty observed the rolling of eyes and heavy sighs. Getting parental consent could be a challenge sometimes. Parents and step-parents either lend their total support or else beat their careless offspring into the ground.

She stayed upbeat despite the teenagers' glum demeanor. "The law says that every company doing postponements must offer a certain number of them to low-income parents. They do that through a non-profit which is good news for you kids."

Molly checked a text message. "When do we got to pay you guys back?"

The woman smiled and gave Molly's hand another reassuring pat making Molly recoil. "It is a wonderful thing about the *Saved By Postponement* option, dear. The surgery and all the monthly maintenance fees are paid for you for the first twenty-four months."

Betty knew the *Saved By Postponement* (SBP) program inside and out since she had volunteered for the organization for the past three years. She first discovered the opportunity while participating in a community reading project. Much of her personal time was given to teenagers and she accepted her new role brimming with eagerness and anticipation. While in her twenties, she had learned the struggles of young adults after being a youth counselor at summer camp and, later, from furnishing troubled youngsters a place to hang out once her own children grew up. Even with several grandchildren, Betty spent two days a week volunteering for the SBP program because it made her feel more vibrant and useful, while providing the ability to save lives.

At last, David spoke, "Who pays for it?"

"Very generous people who want to make postponements available to those who can't afford the service. We call them Angel Donors."

"Kinda trippy that people just give their bank away like that."

Betty went on. "After you accept the contract with SBP, you and one of each of your parents come back here for a consultation. They can describe how all the medical process works."

Curious, David questioned, "Why do we gotta sign a contract?"

Without losing her cheery intensity, Betty answered. "Because if you two can't bring your baby home or take over the payments after two years, we may start looking for another couple to adopt the child."

Molly stared down at her belly and Betty gave Molly's hand a third pat causing the girl to move it down to her lap. "You know honey, sometimes parents are just in a better place after some time, so it's a sensible arrangement." She glanced back and forth between the two adolescents. "So, what do you kids think?"

CHAPTER 21

Nora heard the familiar sound of a cart being wheeled down the hall outside her work station. She stood and poked her head out just as a nurse pushed a crypod unit by. "Sleep tight, little one," she muttered to herself. Picking up a thin pamphlet from her desk, she headed to the family waiting room.

Andy sat stiff in a chair checking his cell phone. He picked up a magazine to try to read, but couldn't fight off his distraction and jumped to his feet and began to pace.

Nora entered, "Andy," and he turned. "Everything went smoothly. Your daughter and wife are both doing well."

He closed his eyes for a moment, then smiled. "We chose a name."

"Names are important," she said, understanding that far beyond what Andy could imagine.

"Adrianna."

"Beautiful," Nora replied. She liked it when the parents named their postponed infants. It was an excellent indicator that demonstrated more connection. Also it meant she didn't need to come up with her own name.

"Can we come and see her in her crypod?" he asked.

She shook her head, "Unfortunately, we don't allow that what with security issues and all. But some people do call to check-in once in a while to see how things are going."

"If it were up to me, I'd take her home right now," he said rubbing the nape of his neck. Nora knew how Andy felt from the time she first met him a few weeks before. When parents disagreed, it always made for strain within the relationship. She had witnessed many heated arguments and hateful accusations between mothers and fathers, and even watched marriages fall apart, which always further complicated things.

Andy made direct eye-contact with her. "Nora, please convince me that she's safe."

Beckoning him to the chairs, she sat down leaving an empty spot between them. "Computers and technicians monitor the crypods around the clock. Many safety precautions have been put in place to ensure the units are fail proof. Redundant systems will engage should there be, say a power failure. And if those backup systems falter or the crypod malfunctions, each unit ensures reanimation."

"What do you mean, ensures reanimation?"

Client Liaisons received periodic script revisions from the marketing department that they were required to use when giving information to parents. However, Nora had spent a long time customizing and formulating her own technical explanations and refused to change, preferring to offer more detailed facts than what the corporate lawyers deemed necessary or were comfortable with. She thought it essential for people to understand the truth about what was going on with their children. "At reanimation the unit is designed to disseminate a specialized solution. This is absorbed by the body at a molecular level warming and aiding in the healthy return to viability."

Still not convinced and a little confused, Andy stared at his oxford shoes.

"This technology is secure. We don't take any risks with these precious lives," She handed him the pamphlet. "Here's some more reading on general crypod maintenance, the reanimation process and our customer service and financial office numbers. Of course, you can phone me directly, anytime."

The new father glanced down at the colorful glossy brochure in his hand. "The agreement said you guys can send babies somewhere else," he said, "I'm not sure I like the fact my daughter might be at an undisclosed location."

"All crypods are kept either here or at our larger Central facility on the east side of Austin."

Andy sighed and Nora bent low enough to get him to look at her. "Don't worry. Adrianna will be well taken care of wherever she stays. You might want some coffee because Arlene's going to be in recovery for a while."

At mid-afternoon, Nora stood in the hallway pretending to be perusing a client file. In reality, she awaited Amisha to scurry off for her daily chocolate fix.

With her coworker gone, Nora slipped into Crypod Holding smiling at the sight of the little individualized cryonic worlds. There wasn't much time until Amisha would reappear, and being seen in there too often made people think Nora didn't have enough work to do which could not be more inaccurate. Toby just needed to be updated.

"I'm going to talk with your mom, tonight," she said while leaning over the infant and stroking the cool Plexiglass. "I promise to do my best."

CHAPTER 22

Still dressed in her work clothes, Nora found the correct address and parked in front of a modest-sized home in an established central Austin neighborhood. She got out of her car and walked towards the door, grateful for the high interlocking tree branches providing a welcomed canopy of shade from the summer afternoon heat. Most of the yards were well kept and trimmed, but the home of Ruben and Sylvia Martinez might benefit from a full Saturday afternoon's worth of work.

Nora rang the doorbell and after twenty seconds, Ruben greeted her, "Hello." She nodded as he held the door open for her. "Down here." They walked in the living room.

"You make any progress?"

He shook his head. A few moments later she heard him hollering up the stairs, "Nora's here."

While waiting, she perused the family photographs of nieces and nephews, a partially finished knitting project and a faux wooden case on the wall holding souvenir spoons. She examined the assortment of teaspoons more closely as her mother had owned one as well. Varied handles with colorful shapes of flowers, animals and lettering from favorite vacation destinations.

On a visit home many years before, Nora discovered her mother's collection hanging in her old bedroom that had been converted into a guest room. No longer were the walls painted aqua and gold as she insisted upon during junior high school, but instead a versatile neutral cream to match the handmade quilt spread across the bed. Nora's memorabilia and childhood possessions set packed in boxes at the edge of the garage.

"You're twenty-eight now, time to grow up and keep your own things," her mother said. "Besides, your father's bent on buying the Wallbeck's pop-up camper. Lord, I'm baffled as to why he wants to start camping at our age, but nevertheless, he needs a place to store the silly thing."

Nora crammed the four stuffed boxes into her car and on the way out of town heaved them into a dumpster behind the Family Dollar.

Both of the Martinezes entered the room. No smiles or pleasantries came from Sylvia. The women had exchanged words in the past so the tension ran deep regardless of Nora's attempt to be polite. "Nice to see you again."

Sylvia ignored the sentiment, sat down, crossed her legs, folded her arms and furrowed her brows.

Ruben tried to cover for his wife's rudeness. "Yes, please sit down. Do you want something to drink?"

Nora shook her head. "I wanted to swing by and talk about your son's situation. I spoke with a former client, Erin, who works in medical research and has a co-worker specifically working on spinal problems."

"And?" said Sylvia.

"And they are getting closer to improving the treatments for these types of birth defects. However things are not quite there, yet."

Toby's mother did not twitch nor blink. "How much longer?"

"It's hard to say exactly. Maybe another year."

"You've been telling us that for the last four."

Nora raised her hands, "I understand. Research takes time to develop and test and then bring to the public."

Ruben kept his mouth shut knowing from experience not to interfere with their conversations.

"There are already surgeries available to help my son. I have read about them on the internet."

"Yes, that's true. But, those procedures may only fix some of his issues. His defect is very severe —"

"You don't know that," Sylvia cut her off mid-sentence. Nora exhaled having been over the same information with this woman numerous times before — each time increasing in difficulty.

"I saw the report. The abnormal development left a portion of his spine not fused properly. Why would you not want to wait for the chance of a complete cure?"

Sylvia swallowed, bit her lower lip and glanced at the ball of blue yarn attached to a half knitted infant sweater in a basket. "There may never be one." A momentary silence filled the air. "I'm tired of waiting for —"

"Yes, I get it," Nora interrupted, her own impatience coming across.

"How could you understand?" Sylvia said. "Are you a mother? Do you have children?"

The bite in the questions took Nora back to the day after her father's funeral.

She had carried her suitcase into the kitchen as her mother held fast to a walker with tennis balls stuck to the front legs.

"I wish you would stay a few days longer," her mother said. "You just got here."

"Sorry. I can't miss my flight back to New Orleans."

Nora's mother pushed herself to a chair and sat down. "Are you ever going to marry and have children?"

Here comes the guilt trip, Nora thought to herself while she buttoned up her jacket.

"Your brother helped so much with your father. I'm not sure where we'd be without him. You'll need someone to care for you when you're old,"

Nora chuckled. "Yeah, like I've done for you and Dad?"

"I didn't mean it that way, honey."

"Sure you did, Mom."

Her mother straightened a crocheted lace doily with a few pats of her fingers. "I realize you're busy with work and what-not. I just miss seeing you."

"I gotta go." Nora gave her mother a cursory hug. "I'll come back when I can."

She told the same thing to Michael while slipping him a check for five hundred dollars. But she had not returned soon enough. Four months later her mother died.

Nora shifted in her seat, unafraid of setting Sylvia straight. "Just because I don't have children doesn't mean I don't understand."

The temperature in the room increased as Sylvia slapped her thighs, "Of course it does. You people freeze the babies all day long. No problem for you. For me —"

"Sylvia," Nora rose to her feet. "If you reanimate your son now, you pretty much guarantee he'll spend his entire life in a wheelchair. I don't need to be a mother to understand how selfish that is."

Jumping up, Sylvia moved forward, her body trembling. "You can't speak like that!"

Ruben attempted an intervention, "Please, let's just —"

"Your company talks all about when the time is right," she waggled a finger in Nora's face. "Well, I'm the parent. And, I will decide when the time is right, not you. This is my child."

Nora clenched her jaw realizing the calm conversation she had intended on could never have happened with this woman. She proved unreasonable and closed-minded having made up her mind before the discussion had even started.

The two women stood staring at each other. "Leave my home!" declared Sylvia in a guttural tone. One minute later, Nora was in her car driving home.

CHAPTER 23

Still upset with Sylvia's inability to overcome her own short-sightedness, Nora opened the last bottle from her wine rack. She made a quick note on her shopping list to pick up a couple more bottles, perhaps a dozen. After kicking off her shoes and pouring herself a glass of chardonnay, she sat down at her kitchen table to reflect on her unsuccessful meeting.

Wishing she had kept her cool for no other reason than for Toby's benefit, it made no sense why on earth Sylvia would consider bringing her son home knowing full well that his life would be filled with adversity. Just waiting a few more years might give him the opportunity for a normal, happy life. *What difference would it make? Go ahead and have more kids, but leave Toby until a real cure was available*, she thought.

The phone rang and Nora rolled her eyes seeing her brother's picture appear on the screen. Cognizant she had to face him at some point, she answered. "Michael."

"What the hell. Why don't you call me back?"

"I'm talking to you now. What do you want?"

He sensed the tension. "What's up with you?"

She exhaled. "Crappy day."

Nora said nothing more so Michael got down to business. "I want you to come to the Fourth of July cookout. I'm making

Dad's famous brisket and Bree's going to attempt Mom's egg salad — although no guarantees there."

"Hey!" Nora heard come from the background followed by a swatting sound.

"I don't think —"

"Aw come on, Sis. You haven't been for a long time. It would be fun. Some of the old gang will be there."

The thought of being around any of those people with perpetual grins and cookie-cutter children made her stomach churn. She didn't understand how Michael could stand to go back every year. "They don't even know me anymore."

"Perfect reason to go."

"I can't —"

"They would love to see you and you could drive down with us. Come on." Her sibling behaved so annoying, sometimes. He would refuse to leave her alone unless she offered some hint of being half-way interested. "Possibly."

"All right then. I'll email you the details."

"Fine." There was an awkward silence. "I have to go," and she hung up.

Michael's phone clattered as he tossed it on the table. "She won't come. She never does," he said to Bree who was cooking dinner, or at least attempting. "Uh, I don't think you're supposed to —" he started as she dumped macaroni into a pan, over-filled it with cold tap water and set it on the stove.

Bree put up her hand to stop him from his criticism. "Did she live through some traumatic childhood or something?"

"Nothing more than anyone else." Michael leaned back in his chair. "You know, friends having fights, neighbors dying, pets getting hit by cars." Bree grimaced at his apathy and stirred the heating water. "Can you get me a..." she gave him a look. "Never mind, I'll get it," and he stood. She raised her hand to stop him then opened the refrigerator and removed a Lone Star. After popping it open, she handed it to him.

"Thanks," he said, unsure of how long she would continue fetching his beer.

"What about friends? I mean was she social?"

"Of course this was before the days of social media or —"

Bree chuckled, "Oh yeah, I forgot. The 'good old days'."

Swallowing a gulp, Michael ignored his typical response when his girlfriend, still not to her mid-thirties yet, chided him about his age. "She had a few close friends, but always acted more reserved than most of them. Never did she like being the center of attention."

Watching the water, Bree asked, "So what about school? Did she struggle?"

"No, not at all. Nora was smart and driven, really focused and did well, way better than I ever did. She almost graduated with a bachelor's degree and had been accepted into med school the following fall. It was a huge deal in our small town and everybody was so proud. We organized a big picnic at home during her spring break before she was to start at UT. But then she completely dropped out."

Raising one eyebrow, Michael watched in amusement as Bree ripped open the white packet with her teeth and added the orange powder along with a heaping spoonful of butter to the boiling water. He held his tongue thinking, *how could any adult not have mastered making macaroni and cheese?* His kids were going to have a field day with her.

"What happened? Why'd she drop out?"

He shrugged. "She'd never say but our parents harbored a lot of disappointed, especially my dad."

"They start treating her bad?"

Michael shook his head. "They were loving people and would have taken her back with open arms, if she came home. I guess she just shoved everything away, including us."

"It isn't healthy to internalize like that," Bree counseled as she pulled a freezer-burned package from the ice box. "Somebody at work lent me a book on kinesiology and I read the first chapter. When we hold stress inside, it can show up in our muscles. Tell her to check that out because they can fix things through stuff like flower essence and acupuncture."

There were certain things Michael had to let slide with his possible future wife as he believed in her admirable intentions. He winced as she began chipping away at frozen hot dogs with a sharp kitchen knife.

"She never moved back to our home town and, in fact, left Texas altogether. I remember her spending time in California, New York, Washington state, Louisiana and wherever else. It seemed like she wanted to run anywhere except for home and only came back for short visits at the holidays and even those got less and less."

One of the dogs shot free and fell like a stone to the floor sliding halfway under the dishwasher. Without blinking an eye, Bree retrieved the fallen soldier, placed him in a bowl alongside three cohorts and popped them all into the microwave oven.

Michael began, "My kids don't like —"

Bree disregarded his second attempted protest. "And then she deserted you when taking care of your sick parents?"

He fetched himself another beer. "Yeah, I told you that before."

Without turning around, Bree said, "I know. But it is good therapy to talk out your family disappointments. And I don't mind listening."

"You read that in a book, too?"

Dismissing the sarcasm in his voice, she responded, "Uh-huh."

"She sent money," he said.

"How'd she end up back here?"

"When postponing was legalized, she got a job with that stupid Postponement company."

"Maybe she spends too much time with those frozen neonates," Bree commented while removing from the microwave the now four wrinkled and shrunken slivers of meat with rock-hard ends.

"They are children," snapped Michael. He snickered realizing the irony in defense of his sister.

Bree shook her head. "Hmm." But she had disengaged from the conversation as she flipped a couple dogs on each of two plates and scooped out the overdone macaroni with a slotted spoon dumping a pile next to the over-cooked meat. After adding a massive helpings of cinnamon applesauce, she put the dishes on the kitchen table.

Michael witnessed a smile of satisfaction grow across her face in serving up nutritious and balanced sustenance to his children. Some protein, some fruit, some dairy and some vegetables, well wait, no vegetable. She walked into the pantry and soon re-emerged with a dusty can of wax beans. Michael closed his eyes and chewed on his lip as she opened the can, jiggled a large portion near the spreading noodles, and sprinkled them with salt.

"Supper!" she yelled out of the room. A few moments later, an eight and eleven year old bound in and sat down. "I've made every kid's favorite things," Bree announced with pride.

The boys looked down at their meal in dismay. "What is this?" the youngest held up a pale yellow wax bean.

"A vegetable," she said putting her fists on her hips.

The children glared at their father and he gave a stern nod for them to eat. The oldest took a bite of the macaroni and cheese. "This is terrible," he complained.

"Yeah," agreed the younger. "It's all mushy and watery."

"Don't be ungrateful," bit Bree.

"My mom cooks way better than you," said the oldest.

Michael sighed accepting that the evening would be a long one.

CHAPTER 24

The Postponement Center hallway buzzed with the activities of an expectant mother being wheeled into surgery, a newborn headed to Crypod Holding, potential parents being escorted to the conference room for a consultation.

Cradling an infant, Nora entered an examination room and greeted her clients.

Tears dropped from Cassandra's eyes as Nora laid the sleeping child into her arms. "She's beautiful," she managed.

The baby stirred, yawned and stretched out quivering hands. Ben pushed his index finger in the minuscule palm and the baby's grip tightened around it. The new father alternated between watching the astonished face of his wife and the face of the precious fresh being for which the wait had seemed like an eternity.

Nora put the standard paperwork on the counter. "I'll need some signatures from both of you and you'll be off on your new life together."

Cassandra, still mesmerized by the child, did not move so Ben walked over. As he skimmed the documents, he noticed something and caught his wife's attention. She rose and carried their new daughter over to see where he was pointing. They both looked up at Nora.

"It says here she was born six years ago," Ben said.

Nora nodded. "Technically, but her legal birth date is only just this morning when she took her first conscious breath. You have yourself a beautiful and healthy newborn."

Cassandra caressed the infant's silken face not caring if the baby had been born a hundred years ago. Her unbearable wait for a child was over.

Fifteen minutes later Nora was back at her desk. These types of circumstances were bittersweet: the adoptive parents being overjoyed at the receiving while the biological parents being devastated by the giving and in this case, not willingly. Nora's head lowered into her hands and she rubbed her eyes. After a few deep breaths, she picked up the phone, dialed and did her best to keep her voice calm.

"Hello Nora."

"Carl. I have —"

He interrupted, "Hey, I was going to call you. My two cousins came through for me so counting your cash and my paycheck this Friday, I'll have enough for the attorney's retainer fee. I finally found one that will take payments so on Monday we're going to meet and start going through all the legal stuff."

She ran fingers through her hair. "Carl. They invoked the provision allowing for the forced adoption."

"No, no. I get paid this —"

"It doesn't matter. You exceeded the grace period."

Unable to fathom her words, he slowed down, "Nora, what do you mean?"

"When there is a breach of contract, the government moves forward. We want to help, but legally it is out of our control."

These were the most difficult conversations and she hated when they came up. "I'm sorry. I explained how serious things could become."

"Is there somebody else I can talk to?"

"Unfortunately, it doesn't work that way. You have no recourse."

"How can they do this? Didn't you tell them I was trying?" Carl pleaded. "Speak to them, again. There's got to be —" His words stopped followed by fifteen seconds of disconcerting silence. "Who got her?"

"We can't reveal that information," said Nora as gently as possible.

She heard gasps on the other end of the line, "But, she's my —"

"I'm very sor —" she began but the phone disconnected. She knew Carl would suffer from anger and guilt for a long time, perhaps years. *Why hadn't he responded more quickly upon learning he had a child?* she thought. Nora took a black marker from her desk and wrote "4301" on the cover of the folder in front of her and placed it in her outbox.

Nora's day had been long and stressful and with only data entry left and no further appointments, she decided to slip out a little early. In the morning she could catch up.

As she walked down the hall, Amisha emerged from a storage area with an opened box of square black batteries. "Apparently your little Toby's going home in a couple days," she said. "I saw the mother called this morning and scheduled through central client services. Tough break." Nora's jaw slackened. She felt like she had been slugged in the gut.

CHAPTER 25

Even though Nora knew the day would come when Toby would be going home, she had tried in earnest to have it not be so soon. She turned around and entered Crypod Holding and with a slow, dread-filled walk, she went to Toby's unit. Fighting back tears, she glided her hand across the chilled surface, staring at the little life on hold inside. It would be a life filled with potential repercussions; a victim of his mother's ignorance. "Forgive me, Toby," she whispered.

Ducking out the back door, Nora walked to her vehicle watching the protesters that had once again returned to the front of TPC. There appeared to be an increasing number as the exact anniversary of the legalization of postponement services approached.

The picketer signs were colorful hand-creations purporting claims Nora believed to be ridiculous.

SAVE THE BABIES
NO PREGNANCY UNLESS YOU WANT A CHILD
#BANPOSTPONEMENTS
OVERTURN PLACER V. GRASSMEN

As Nora drove slowly to avoid hitting anyone, her anger began to overtake her sadness and she fought the urge to mow a few of them down. Though her windows were rolled up tight, she could still hear their shallow statements.

"What you're doing here is immoral," screamed the woman with bright red hair. "Postponing is selfish!" Nora sensed that woman was the leader — the instigator, since she never missed any days when the demonstrators walked. What she cried out, her blind followers repeated, shaking their fists. "Postponing is selfish!"

Besides the red head, Nora recognized certain picketers from passing through them so many times. Among the minions, the blonde-haired, blue-eyed young woman had exhibited more boldness over the weeks. At first remaining in the back carrying a sign with the words, POSTPONEMENT = PROFITS. Now confident to join in with the chanting and fist waving, "There are consequences for what you are doing," she shouted as Nora's car proceeded through the mob. "You care more about profits than you do about babies."

Nora looked at the blonde woman who seemed surprised at her own timbre and pleased to provoke a positive reaction from the red head and some others. "You tell her, Emma!" They cheered and patted her on the back, then all began repeating, "Life over money. Life over money."

Nora had always managed to ignore protester accusations before, but for some reason, Emma's claim, "You care more about profits than you do about babies," hit her like an anvil meeting its mark. Maybe it was because of Nora's earlier conversation with Carl and the loss of his daughter or perhaps it was the stupidity of Sylvia Martinez' decision to reanimate their son prematurely. More likely it stemmed from the disappointment of knowing she would not see Toby in his crypod every day. Emma might as well have plunged a blade deep into Nora's heart.

Once home, Nora changed into her running clothes. Running was the one activity that could clear her mind and burn off the frustrations of the day. She ran further and harder than she had for a long while. The playground was busy and the baseball diamonds packed with after-school practices and games.

Nora jogged by a soccer field where kids clamored to control a ball. Not paying attention to where she was going, she stepped into a pothole and her ankle twisted resulting in a stumble to the ground. She bumped her head on a nearby metal bench. Glancing around, Nora realized no one saw her go down.

Dragging herself up, she lifted her pant leg to examine her scraped and bloodied knee. The bump on her head felt tender but thankfully oozed no blood.

The children ran and fell as well. They bounced up and ran some more, chasing and kicking the ball.

After a rest, Nora took a drink of cool water from her bottle, rose to her feet, and limped home from her injury. The goose-egg on her head was growing.

CHAPTER 26

Still in her running clothes, Nora opened her freezer and removed a package of tender green peas. Not bothering to close the door, she eased herself into a kitchen chair and placed the bag to the bump on her head. Ah, the coolness. How soothing.

On her table, pushed to the side, were the new notebook and pens, and the unopened book *Creating Stories Kids Will Love*.

Nora sat motionless for a long time while staring inside the freezer. Her mind meandered from a barrage of thoughts to the emptiness of nothing at all.

In a sudden movement she jumped up hurling the vegetable bag into the sink where it burst allowing half-thawed peas to roll out. She swung open the door to the refrigerator as well and stood back looking at the disarray of bottles, jars, and containers.

She began removing and stacking everything on the counters and into the sinks. Nora dumped the expired, shriveled, moldy and unidentifiable. Having always disliked this household task, her mother always employed it as an effective punishment while growing up.

When both the upper and lower lay barren, she took a sponge and spray cleanser and cleaned every inch of shelf and drawer space. Her fingers grew pink and raw from the furious scrubbing. Beads of perspiration formed on her forehead and her breathing increased from the forced physical labor.

Nora saw that everything appeared spotless and shiny and she wiped her sweaty brow with a paper towel. Then she returned all the salvageable items placing them in perfect alignment. Frozen food was packed in neat and tidy.

Once everything was back, Nora admired all the renewed organization. The soy sauce required one half turn so the label faced front. Everything was arranged in its best place. She slammed the doors closed, dropped the bag of soggy peas into the trash and washed the remaining ones down the disposal. They swirled away in the flow of lukewarm tap water.

She used a folding step stool to reach in the back of a high cupboard retrieving a three-ringed yellow binder. After getting down, she set it on her counter and brushed off the accumulated dust and leftover flour from the cover. A small smile donned her face as she reminisced about how much her mother relied on this collection of recipes.

Nora began flipping through the pages. Most pages exhibited evidence from years of use and abuse and were decorated with splotches of red and gray splashes and spills. Her mother had been wise to slip each piece of paper into its own clear plastic page protector.

She recognized many dishes her family enjoyed. Remembrances of her mother tricking her and her brother to eat the grotesque vegetable came to mind as she perused the recipe for Broccoli Casserole. Other warm memories surfaced with the titles of Swedish Apple Pudding and Sweet Jalapeño Cornbread. Nora chuckled upon seeing a recipe called Prune Crock — solely earmarked for her father and no one else in the house dared to touch that concoction.

Michael took care of all the sorting in their parents' house after they died. Nora feigned too busy to help. "I just started this new job and I can't get any time off." After a few protests, he sighed and accepted her response.

Five months later, she received a small Federal Express box from Michael containing the "Collins' Family Cookbook" and a scribbled post-it note. "You've got to come home for the rest. Love Mikey." But she never went back to her small childhood town.

Nora blinked her watery eyes and wished she had remembered to stop for wine because she could use a glass or three. Instead, she settled for one of two Lone Star's discovered at the rear of the refrigerator during her OCD cleaning foray. A couple Christmas Eves ago, Michael arrived on her doorstep holding a twelve-pack.

"Why are you here?" Nora asked.

"It's Christmas Eve," he slurred. "Can't I be with my sister?"

Noticing his truck parked crooked in her driveway, she realized he had already consumed half of the cans of and who knew what else. She exhaled and brought him inside. "Where are your kids?"

"Mother's year."

After getting past her irritation for him showing up unannounced, she ended up listening to his woes about being a single father, hating his job, and missing fishing trips with their father. After he passed out on her couch, she called a taxi and paid the driver a hundred dollars to make sure Michael got home safe.

The Lone Star fizzed when opened and she took a swig. Her face scrunched, she didn't like the flavor, but it would have to do.

Nora continued turning pages until she found the desired page. The tiny lettering was faded but still visible. A date on the top of "Mama's Butter Cupcakes" recipe read "September 1919." She did not possess many memories of her grandparents as they lived far from Texas in New Hampshire. During the few times their family could afford a visit, she recalled the savory and amazing homemade desserts created by her grandmother. Never had there been a retail cupcake to rival Mama's, ever.

Nora finished her drink, surprised at how fast it had gone down, and opened the second. She began to gather the necessary ingredients from her pantry and various cupboards to prepare the cake batter: flour, baking powder, confectioner sugar, granulated sugar, salt and vanilla. Butter, milk and eggs were now a cinch to find in her sanitized refrigerator. However, the cream cheese rested at the bottom of the garbage after having turned green and furry, and she didn't keep heavy whipping cream on hand. Nora considered her half-finished second beer. A quick trip to the supermarket would work and she could also pick up something decent to drink.

Almost an hour later she reentered her kitchen carrying a brown-handled paper bag. Out came the fresh cream cheese, the carton of whipping cream, and a can of Betty Crocker Rich & Creamy Chocolate Frosting. Proud of herself for making cupcakes from scratch, she decided to settle for convenience on the topping.

Out of a smaller paper sack came an impulse purchase from the liquor store next to the market. The bottle of Stag's Leap 2006 Cask 23 Cabernet Sauvignon had cost well into three figures, not including the cents. Uncorking it, she filled an oversized goblet reserved for special occasions — that notably never came. The first sip tasted juicy and sweet, but not too sweet. It was well worth the price, way better than bitter beer, and a luxurious splurge for tonight.

Nora got down to business. In twenty-five minutes the mixture was poured into liners and two glasses of the extravagant cabernet had disappeared. The pan slipped in the pre-heated oven and the timer was engaged.

While the little delicacies baked, she started a load of laundry then worked on her laptop at the kitchen table. It had been a while since she signed into the website and checked her bank account. Direct deposit and automatic payments made it easy to not worry or fuss with finances.

Feeling a bit wobbly on her feet now, she pulled the goodies from the oven. Nora heeded the additional handwritten directions, added by her mother, to immediately remove the miniature cakes to avoid overcooking that resulted in drying them out. She transferred the mini-cakes to a rack. The irresistible aroma infused the room triggering her saliva glands and making her mouth water.

During the cooling process, she completed folding piles of clothing that had not seen the inside of a washing machine in a long time.

Each individual dessert was now iced into a circular chocolaty tip. Nora glided the butter knife across her tongue finishing the smooth final spoonful of artificial chocolate, trans-fat and preservatives. Simply delightful.

The hunt began for the sprinkles. Annually she volunteered to bring cookies for client appreciation day so knew they must be somewhere. After acquiring another glass of adult fermented grape juice and a ten minute search, the pesky bottle reappeared hiding behind canned organic garbanzo beans.

A rainbow of sugary sprinkles always made cupcakes appear festive and delicious. Tempted to try just one, she resisted and moved the full dozen treats to a Tupperware container and snapped on the lid.

Taking a moment to polish off the last of her expensive indulgence, she switched off the lights and staggered out of the kitchen. The blue night light in the wall plug illuminated and the digital readout on the stove glowed 3:37 a.m.

CHAPTER 27

Outside TPC, the protesters were back. Emma stood at the edge of the group with a couple of fresh recruits. She had conjured up a new sense of confidence and purpose as she pointed to where the newcomers may and may not walk and praised them for their creative sign-making.

The reinforcement of the comment Emma had made the day before to one of the TPC employees had given her a renewed focus of participating in the fight. Her parents continued coercing her to be more active in social justice issues. "Stand for something," Emma's father railed before launching into one of his repeated stories of peaceful protests during his own college years.

Emma's mother and father would be proud that she was doing something worthy and meaningful, and saving babies was the perfect cause. Her five older siblings all graduated from expensive universities and were finding success in the medical, educational and engineering fields. As the youngest, she struggled. Frequent changes in her declared major resulted in the insistence by her parents to pick and stick with one. She finally settled on business administration. Not one hundred percent thrilled with the classes, Emma managed to maintain decent grades with only three semesters left before graduation.

Emma noticed Nora's vehicle located at the street curb. Although appreciating the persistence of the employees that crossed the picket line daily, she couldn't understand how these people did what they did just to earn a living. A hotness welled in her stomach thinking of how they condoned and enabled putting human lives on hold merely for parents' convenience.

The red head placed her hand on Emma's back. "You say what's in your heart, sweetie."

Feeling empowered, the young woman said, "I will, Jillian," and pushed herself to the front readying once again to walk along Nora's car window. Maybe today she might make her point powerful enough to convince that one employee to think again about how she puts food on her table. Emma felt convinced she was making a difference.

Nora's Honda sat to the side of the road beyond the TPC parking lot spending a few minutes gathering herself and drinking from a travel mug of strong coffee. The caffeine plus the aspirin she swallowed earlier was helping mute the consequences of last night's activities.

She observed the protesters walking back and forth with signs chanting, "It's life, not convenience. It's life, not convenience." Jillian, the red head, led a mob towards a pregnant teenage girl who walked from the bus stop to The Postponement Center. They surrounded her like ants on one of Nora's cupcakes.

"Don't buy into their lies," they told her as their intensity swelled. "Your baby has the right to live now."

Nora inferred something about her dedication, her being there almost every day and remaining engaged with what she believed to be right. There could be no disrespect about that even though Nora vehemently opposed the method of delivery. After finishing her coffee, she drove unhurried through the crowd.

The young blonde woman caught Nora's eye and called out, "Babies deserve life!"

TPC enforced strict corporate guidelines about not speaking to, engaging in, or provoking picketers in any way. Over the years she had been almost faithful in following those rules. Yet there was something about this day and this woman that Nora chose to no longer ignore. She stopped and lowered her window.

The other demonstrators saw what was happening and swarmed closer in excitement bobbing their posters and calling out their single-minded statements. Nora and Emma held intense, steady eye-contact.

"You should be saving these babies," Emma stated in an authoritative voice.

With more control than anticipated and without dropping her stare, Nora responded, "I am." The two women's eyes remained locked for a few seconds longer as the mass grew more riled up.

Expecting an onslaught of accusations or a well thought through rebuttal, Emma stayed silent, her eyes falling away. The sense of a minor victory overcame Nora. She had made a point! Perhaps she had depleted a little wind from the woman's sails. *How naïve to assume she knew anything about life at her young age. For certain she deserved to be put in her place*, Nora thought.

Nora rolled her window back up, entered the lot and parked her car. As she hung a backpack strap over her shoulder, she disappeared into the lobby and right away witnessed more yelling. At the reception desk stood a man in his early fifties who was unleashing his anger on Christine and JC, his arms flailing. "You're all incompetent."

Despite him towering over her, Christine did not rise hoping to not create a more hostile environment. "Sir, we have a notarized document —"

"I did not sign anything," the man shouted pushing his index finger almost into her chest. "That bitch forged my signature and you are responsible for —"

"Hey now, you need to calm down," said JC, stepping forward.

The man refused. "Don't you tell me what to do! You'd better get your arrogant lawyers ready, because I'm gonna battle this company till I get my kid back."

Nora slipped unnoticed through the door into the hallway.

CHAPTER 28

Nora entered the conference room carrying a file. *Christine forgot to replace the flowers*, she thought, seeing three fallen rose petals lying on the table. Will and Monica Walters turned their heads and ceased whispering, confusion written on both faces.

"What's going on, Nora?" Will questioned.

She sat down across from the worried couple noticing the mother's hand resting upon an unblemished blue diaper bag adorned with green elephants and yellow giraffes.

"Why'd they bring us in here?" asked Monica. "Last time we went straight to the other room. Is something wrong?"

"Yes." Nora's words sounded obligatory and monotone. Part of getting through that day. "Not long after the reanimation, your son suffered a congenital heart problem."

"What?" Will said in disbelief.

Monica put her hand to her mouth, "Oh my god."

Nora swallowed and forced her emotions to stay intact as she saw the horror on the woman's face. "I apologize. He didn't make it."

Tears welled in Monica's eyes as a few moments of silence filled the room. "We never should have done this again." she said, desperate to find a logical reason although there was no logic to find.

Will leaned forward glaring at Nora, perspiration instantly formed on his forehead. "Is this your people's fault?"

"Will, this is not something our process caused."

"How can you be sure?"

Monica looked at her husband, salty droplets beginning to run down her cheeks. "Maybe it was me. I didn't know I was pregnant at first and —"

"Conditions present at the original birth simply progress at their natural pace once reanimation occurs. These issues —"

"You sound like a damn robot," Will blurted out.

Nora paused a moment then continued. "These issues can sometimes take years to develop in a child and other times become apparent in just a few minutes."

Monica's head fell forward into her hands as she began to sob. Will put his arm around her.

"I understand this is difficult." Nora slid a paper and pen across the table. "You're afforded forty-eight hours for optional parental viewing with the choice of either cremation or physical burial. We'll need your signatures instructing us how you would like to handle your son's remains." She stood. "I'm sorry. Take as long as you'd like. You can check in with the receptionist when you're finished and she will make the appropriate arrangements and give you some information and phone numbers for support groups."

The couple were no longer paying attention to Nora mired in their grief and she left the room. An unavoidable tear fell and she wiped it away while walking down the hall to her work station. *Why did that have to happen, today, of all days,* she thought.

Her phone rang, she answered and listened. Nora closed her eyes for a long moment. "I'll be there in twenty minutes, then."

CHAPTER 29

The TPC doctor and CEO stood staring out one of his corner office floor to ceiling windows to a beautiful wooded preserve and small lake. Plaques and framed certificates decorated the walls along with photographs of his wife and adult children.

These were the times when he could not wait to retire, yet that was still years away. Oh, to enjoy every single home game of his beloved San Antonio Spurs and take his family on overpriced, exotic vacations. His wife had been pestering him about a month-long cruise to Europe.

The doctor shifted his view out of his second window that faced the front of TPC. He could see the picketers marching on the sidewalk. Will and Monica Walters, the couple Nora spoke with earlier headed to their vehicle. Will's arm encircled his wife's waist, supporting her. The demonstrators yelled something at them and at first, he waved them off. Then, he and his wife exchanged words and walked over to the group.

"Great," muttered Dr. Thompson. All he needed was more bad press. He watched as the protesters surrounded the grieving couple, joined hands and bowed their heads to pray.

He folded his arms and tried to select the best strategy for handling the impending conversation. Nora Collins definitely met the criteria of a high maintenance employee. Quite frequently she barreled across the threshold with parents and exhibited an excessive obsession with the neonates. The threat of or an actual write-up usually pushed her back in line for a few months although the number of times he counseled Nora almost embarrassed him. Yet, was he to fire his top sales person? Nora's numbers proved her as integral for The Postponement Center's success. The knowledge gained during her tenure had developed her into a valuable asset for the growing business. The majority of the clientele seemed to like her odd, no-nonsense way.

Entering the waiting area outside of her boss's office, Marcia told Nora to go on in because he was expecting her. Nora's hands were clammy and she fought back agitation having no idea why she had been summoned to meet with him — well, maybe she did.

As soon as she took in Dr. Thompson's face, his expression indicated there was a problem. He exhaled and pursed his lips and motioned for her to sit down across from him at his oversized mahogany desk.

"And here we are again, Nora," he said as he placed a paper in front of her. "Look familiar?"

She immediately recognized the document and rubbed her palms on her pants. *Could this day get any worse?* "Of course," she answered. "It's the paperwork from a client when she picked up her son a few weeks ago."

Dr. Thompson slid a file towards her. "This is the father's actual signature. Are these anything alike?"

Nora took a cursory glance, "She had a notarized —"

"You've worked here long enough to follow protocol," he interrupted. "Now this man is threatening to sue because you didn't properly verify documentation."

Keeping her eyes on a desk photograph of a young boy dressed in a Little League outfit, she mumbled, "But, the moth —"

"I can't hear you," he said.

Nora felt as if she was being scolded by a parent and spoke louder. "The mother was in an abusive situation."

"We don't know that."

"But I saw bruises and —"

"That is not our responsibility," he said, a slight crack in his voice.

What an ass, she thought. *Here he sits in his Taj Mahal office never dealing with any day-to-day crap with the clients.* The last time he reprimanded her was a few months back after she helped an expectant woman. Nora went with her to talk with her husband in an attempt to convince him to agree to a postponement rather than an abortion. He refused and called complaining that TPC employees shouldn't be interfering in his private decisions.

Nora's gaze fell back down to the floor. "Can I go?"

However, her boss was not finished. "Are you giving clients money, again?"

"Of course not," lied Nora knowing it would do her no good to venture an explanation.

"And someone witnessed you this morning provoking one of the protesters. You are not to speak with them, ever."

Dr. Thompson sat back in his chair, folded his hands and then leaned forward again. "We've discussed all these things on more than one occasion. You have an excellent track record with bringing business in, but you cannot continue to break the rules. I've tried to be patient with you, but if you insist on ignoring our policies, I will have no other choice but to let you go and I really don't want to do that. Do you understand?"

She did not speak.

"Nora?" he said.

"Yes."

"You must not get involved in the clients' personal business. No giving out money, no going to their homes, no talking to protesters and no making friends with former clients. This is a professional company, not a charity organization. Please don't let your emotional attachment to these neonates control your judgment."

Sensing it best to depart now, Nora stood and walked to the door, but before leaving, she turned to face him. "A few minutes ago, I had to tell a couple that the child they had waited on for three years was dead. Do you have any idea how hard that is?"

He closed his eyes for a moment and kept his voice calm. "You know that's part of the job."

Nora said nothing further and exited the office.

CHAPTER 30

Nora walked down the hall adjusting her shirt as perspiration rolled down her back — she just had to get through this day.

She opened the conference room door where two innocent-faced young kids, that couldn't be more than a week past eighteen, sat dwarfed by the table. Nora said nothing, took a seat and began fiddling with her tablet.

The boy squirmed after a minute of silence and said, "Hi, I'm LeVon and this is my girlfriend, Tisha." Another awkward silence permeated the air while Nora remained pre-occupied scrolling through screens. "So, we want to go ahead and sign up for the postponement thing."

Nora raised her head up for the first time. She attempted to act normal, but found herself far from it and was quite abrupt. "You crossed the picket line?"

"Yeah," said Tisha.

"Why?"

She looked at her boyfriend and then back at Nora. "Uh, 'cuz we still wanna do it."

Drawing in a long breath and exhaling it, Nora's words emerged rote and stiff. Any internal emotions void on her face. "I'm a Client Liaison. Your primary contact throughout the entire process from beginning to end: applications, scheduling, procedures and maintenance..."

She continued with the presentation perfected over the previous seven years not caring that she was speaking way above her clients' ability to understand. No invitation for questions was offered. "...We do all we can to ensure the safe keeping of our infants," Nora finished.

The couple frowned at each other about the onslaught of information and Nora's disengaged manner.

"Do you even like your job, Miss Collins?" asked Tisha.

Nora stared at the young girl.

CHAPTER 31

That awful day was coming to an end when Nora walked into Crypod Holding and observed preparation for a transfer order.

Amisha held in her hand a silver canister similar looking to a slender thermos. She screwed it in place at the head of a crypod. Locking a specialized square battery into a slot on the side, she punched some keys on a pad, and disconnected two twenty volt plugs from an outlet. After viewing the unit for half a minute confirming all functions transitioned over to local power, she set the crypod on a cart.

"Amisha, I know your daughter has dance class tonight. Why don't you let me do this?"

"She does and I'm running late. But, if Dr. Thompson finds out —"

"It will be fine. He's already left for the day."

Amisha pinched her chin. "It would be nice for her not to have to miss another lesson."

Treating her coworker to a rare smile, Nora waved her hand, "I don't mind at all."

"I would so much appreciate it," Amisha conceded and handed over a printout. "Here are the ones going. Transport will be here in an hour. Thank you. I'll see you tomorrow." The Crypod tech snatched her belongings and ran out of the room.

Nora understood how to do the preparations as efficiently as Amisha and she scanned the list, walked to a shelf to collect three recharged batteries and began prepping the remaining crypods. She made six trips back and forth wheeling individual carts from Crypod Holding to Pick Up and Delivery.

Glancing at her watch fifty-five minutes later, she pushed the opener by the back door making the metal door roll up. It was almost dark and the chilly inside air began to intermingle with the warm evening breeze. Nora leaned against the wall.

Soon a windowless, unmarked van backed in and two men jumped out wearing polo shirts with the TPC logo and Transportation Specialist embroidered on the upper left side.

"Haven't seen you in a while," said Brent when he saw Nora.

"Just helping out," she replied as he smiled then pointed to the second man swinging open the vehicle's back doors.

"That's Jimmy. He's new. Showing him the routine." Jimmy and Nora gave each other a polite nod and she stepped back. "So, only the five?"

"Yup."

The veteran carefully passed one unit at a time up to the rookie who placed them in the rear. "You gotta keep these things level. Can't tip 'em sideways." The newbie slid the crypods on thick shelves, taking a moment to peer inside the first one. He blinked and tilted his head but said nothing.

Brent hopped in the back to show his protégé how to secure the costly cargo. "These straps cross here and you tighten them like this."

They finished their work as Nora stood, hands clasped in front of her. With all the units secured, Jimmy slammed the doors and Brent walked over for her signature on an automated handheld device. "Should we close the door from outside?"

"No. I've got a few things to haul out," she said.

"Need some help?"

She gave Brent a half smile, "Thanks, not necessary. It's not much."

"Okay, have a good night." He got into the van and pulled out.

Back at her work station, Nora glanced over her shoulder. No one was there. Jiggling the mouse reactivated the computer and she entered some keystrokes before switching everything off and leaving with her purse.

She poked her head into the security office. Brady sat at a long desk behind several screens monitoring various areas around The Postponement Center property. He held a fishing magazine on his lap. JC perused his phone catching up on baseball scores.

"Hey guys," she said. They both looked up.

"You still here?" JC said observing the time on the wall clock.

"I gave Amisha a hand with the Central shipment. But, they're gone now."

Brady squinted at one of the monitors. "Those knuckleheads left the door open."

"Really? Oh. I'll go out the back way and make sure it gets closed."

"Sure?" he asked.

"Of course. Besides, I have a special surprise for you two back in the break room."

With broad grins, the men both rose to their feet. "You know the way to a man's heart," said Brady making her chuckle and head the opposite direction.

A few minutes later, Nora drove into the open back entrance and exited her car. She disappeared into a darkened corner of Pick Up and Delivery, soon re-emerging pushing the sixth cart. A crypod on top.

Opening the back door of the vehicle, she lifted it into the backseat, belted it in as best she could, and covered it with a lime green blanket. Next to it she put the full backpack.

Nora reversed out of the loading area, then got out momentarily to tap in a code on the exterior keypad causing the door to lower.

CHAPTER 32

Nora's hands trembled despite squeezing the steering wheel until her knuckles lost color. Her heart throbbed as she headed away from TPC. Jumbled thoughts rifled through her mind. *What had I done? Was I crazy? Maybe I should go back.*

Nora needed to kill some time unable to reach her destination until after midnight. A stiff alcoholic drink sounded appropriate, but she settled for a strong coffee instead.

Finding a space as far from the entrance as possible, she changed out of her TPC clothing and pulled on jeans and a plain tan tee-shirt she had placed on her passenger seat that morning. She locked her car and went into the bustling establishment.

Groups of friends huddled around low tables whispering and laughing. Young couples engaged with their phones as opposed to each other. Readers and writers, reading and writing. So much happening, everyone living their individual lives and not one of them knew what Nora had done or who lay in her back seat.

Sitting on a hard wooden chair by the window, she rested her chin in the crook of her intertwined fingers gazing with unblinking eyes through the water-spotted glass. A thirty foot high sprawling canopy of deep purple blooms draped over her Honda with its precious contents inside.

Long after the employees collapsed the outer forest-green umbrellas and began stacking chairs for easier floor cleaning, she received a polite apology and a request to leave. She swallowed the final sip of cold black coffee from her extra-large cup unsure if her jittery hands were still from her earlier actions or a result of the massive dose of caffeine she had nursed for three hours.

Nora walked across the parking lot, her clothes and hair reeking of smoky fresh-ground beans. The headlights from the street traffic blazed bright, almost blinding with the contrasting dark skies. A growl came from Nora's abdomen as dinner had long been forgotten. She would need to find something to eat. Her watch indicated it was after eleven. Only another hour until she planned to arrive. She must be inconspicuous.

Driving was something to keep her hands and mind occupied. She cruised random Austin neighborhoods being cautious of any sudden stops or sharp turns that might upset the crypod in the back. It had been fastened in well, but still she did not want to take any chances.

Nora passed by the University of Texas campus she had attended almost three decades before. Most memories of tests and reports had long been tucked away. The narrow roads in front of sororities and fraternity houses seemed familiar. They were elegant and distinguished buildings, some having been built in the thirties and forties, with well-kept landscaping and mature trees.

An array of new vegan and healthy eating restaurants and bars promoting local brews lined the streets. Nora recognized one sandwich shop she had spent many late nights in. It still looked the same except for the new window decal touting Free Wifi. A few summer school students studied inside, earbud wires hanging across their chests and faces buried in laptops.

While recalling her own cramming for assignments, a police car behind her switched on flashing red and blue lights. "Oh shit," she said seeing the reflection in her rearview mirror and pulling over to the curb.

A quick peek to the back made her thankful to have covered the crypod. She touched the radio knob turning on some music loud enough to mask the gurgle emitting from the unit.

Nora lowered her window as the uniformed man approached. He stood back a couple of feet, one hand resting on his holstered gun and the other shining a flashlight at her. She squinted blocking the glare with her hand. "License, registration and insurance, please."

As she retrieved the requested items from her purse and the glove compartment, he flashed the light into the rear seat. She grit her teeth and felt sick to her stomach, worried he would discover her secret. "Did I do something wrong, sir?" He turned his attention back to her, as she hoped he would.

After handing him the papers, he examined her driver's license. "Have you been drinking, Ms. Collins?"

"Only coffee."

"Be right back," he said and walked back to confer with his squad car's onboard computer, his high beams streaming through the back window of her vehicle. She stared straight forward, not moving, barely breathing.

When he returned, he handed back her documents seeming to have altered his attitude. He smiled, a kind smile, Nora thought. "I followed you for ten minutes. You were going fifteen miles under the posted speed limit."

"I'm sorry, Officer Lloyd," she said noticing his name tag. The hair graying at his temples made her guess they both were close to the same age. "Just doing a little reminiscing."

"You graduate from UT?" he asked.

"I went for almost four years, but didn't finish."

"Ah. I went here too. Born and raised in Austin. Got a football scholarship." She tilted her head figuring crime must be in a lull with all his niceties — of course, it was a Tuesday. He leaned down in a friendly way. "You stayed here as well. What do you do?"

Certain he was a pleasant man, Nora didn't feel like chitchatting, but also didn't want to be rude and get a ticket, or worse yet, have him inquire as to what lie under that blanket. "I'm a teller."

"My sister has a job in a bank. Which one?" he inquired, acting genuinely interested.

She answered with the first one that came to mind, "Chase."

Amused, the man nodded, "That's where she works and I bank there as well. Which branch?"

Nora coughed and took a gulp from her water bottle. "Excuse me. I'm actually still in training so I'm not sure where I'll end up." The small talk increased her anxiety and she rubbed moisture from her forehead. Perhaps he'd already called for backup and was stalling until they arrived. Soon she would be arrested. *That is silly*, she scolded herself. No way could anyone have discovered what she had done. Nothing would be reported, not yet, at least.

The police officer stared at her after having asked another question that she missed. "I'm sorry, what?"

"Are you feeling okay, Ms. Collins? Your hands are trembling." She licked her dry lips. "Oh, I haven't eaten all day, bad me."

"You seem awfully pale and you're sweating up a storm. Are you sure you're not coming down with something?"

"It's just this humidity. You know, Texas in the summer." Nora forced a chuckle and a fraudulent grin.

"I could escort you to urgent care if you'd like. Wouldn't want you passing out on the way," he said, not convinced.

Was he trying to pick her up? "No, I'll be fine. Thanks though."

"All right then. Please be aware of your speed. Going too slow can cause accidents too."

"Yes sir," said Nora, shifting her car back into gear. "Thank you for not giving me a ticket."

He smirked, "No problem. Us Bevo's gotta stick together." She smiled knowing he likely remained a loyal UT fan flying a canvas flag of Bevo, the Longhorn Steer mascot, on every game day.

"Good luck with the new job," he said stepping back. "I'll be on the lookout for you."

Nora nodded as she rolled up her window. "I bet you will," she muttered while accelerating up to the twenty-five miles per hour reflected on the street sign. The clock read 12:36 a.m. so she drove to the pre-chosen location, cringing at the site.

CHAPTER 33

The rundown two-story motel was in dire need of some maintenance. The chipped stucco screamed for a new paint job and several steps were cracked and broken. All the rooms had exterior access and only a half dozen cars dotted the unswept and pot-holed parking lot.

Nora pulled into a spot near the "ice." The "off" side of the neon sign burned out. She locked the car door and entered the postage-stamp-sized lobby.

No one stood behind the dull formica counter, so she tapped a nearby bell and a moment later, a tired, scowling elderly desk clerk shuffled from the back. He set down his half-read novel, Stephen King's *Cujo*, and widened his eyes at her.

"I need a room for a few nights," said Nora.

He grunted, put his hands on the keyboard and typed at a snail-like pace. "First floor okay?"

"Perfect," she said.

"ID and credit card."

"I'm paying cash."

The clerk sighed without looking up. "Still need an ID."

Nora dropped a twenty dollar bill in front of him. "Will that work?"

Without looking, he scooped it up and stuffed it into his pocket. "Perfect," he mocked.

Minutes later, Nora unlocked the marred door and flipped on the light to survey the room. An attempt to mask some kind of odor, perhaps cigarette smoke, created an overpowering chemical-laden lemon scent. The assault on her senses forced a harsh rubbing of her nose. The room was far from luxurious, but it must do.

Handling first things first, the old-fashioned floral bedspread was yanked off and thrown against the wall before putting her duffle bag, backpack and white paper sack on the bed. Using both palms, she pushed down on a rickety red desk making sure of its sturdiness then she wiped it down with some disinfectant wipes she had brought.

After disappearing for a few moments, she returned carrying the draped unit and placed it on the desktop. Closing and bolting the door, she returned her attention to her backpack. She rearranged several six-inch silver canisters and removed two of the four-inch square black batteries, plugging one into a wall charger.

Nora unpacked her clothes hanging some and placing the rest in dresser drawers she had jimmied open. Every freshly laundered shirt and skirt, tee-shirt and pair of jeans, even sweater and sweatshirt, had been retrieved from either the rear of her closet or the storage bins in her second bedroom. An inconsequential sense of accomplishment came from knowing her somewhat healthy eating habits and frequent jogging kept her fit enough to still squeeze into the old clothing.

Her green zippered bathroom bag went next to the discolored sink. The corner of the mirror was shattered and mildew lined the shower grout. Her quality expectations had been low, yet not quite to that level. However, her discomfort did not matter as a more important reason for being there existed.

Opening the food bag, Nora sat on the bed to eat her salad and banana. Any escaped nuts from her yogurt and granola were quickly discarded.

Thirty minutes later, she laid on the lumpy bed in her pajamas facing the crypod, the green blanket pulled back. Everything in the room appeared muted in the darkness except for an eerie blue glow on her face and the outline of Toby. A faint gurgling came from the unit.

He slept peaceful, like a butterfly awaiting to be born into an angry world. But he needed to have the opportunity to fully spread his wings.

Her mind raced considering every possible scenario that might occur once Dr. Thompson found Toby missing. She might end up in jail. Perhaps she could still take him back and explain her mistake, but no, she wasn't running away — not this time.

Desperate to fall asleep, she rolled over and stared at the blinking fire alarm on the ceiling. She began counting between each green flash: thirty seconds, twenty-five seconds, thirty-five seconds. Foul words permeated the paper thin walls as the couple next door erupted into a terrible argument. Upon one of many trips to the restroom, the light illuminated a massive cockroach scurrying down the bathtub drain. She groaned and plugged it hoping the disgusting creature would not reappear from the overflow.

After tossing most of the night, Nora realized she had indeed fallen to sleep when an abrupt pound on the motel room door jolted her awake.

CHAPTER 34

Nora's watch read 11:32. She had overslept. There was another sharp rat-ta-tat-tat along with a woman's voice, "Housekeeping."

The door opened two inches before catching on the flimsy metal latch and Nora bolted to the door as the housekeeper tried to enter. "No thank you. I don't need anything. Please, don't come back." The woman left mumbling something in Spanish.

With a sigh of relief, she returned to Toby's crypod feeling more reassured as she watched the white mist still in circulation. She took one of the two extra batteries and slipped it into a second slot on the unit but no green light showed. Pulling the dead battery back out, she plugged it into the wall charger but nothing happened. Frowning, Nora inserted another full battery and put the depleted one on to recharge.

Shaking her head, she turned the bad black square over in her hands scolding herself for not taking more. She must figure something out and she dropped it in the waste can with a jarring clunk.

Nora picked up her cell phone and dialed a familiar number. "Hi Erin," she said, doing her best to keep her voice sounding casual.

"Hey you, how's it going?"

"Going well, thanks." Nora began pacing as Erin launched into the description of a custom jewelry party she was hosting at her home along with plenty of wine and cheese and how much fun it would be.

"This Friday evening?"

"Uh-huh."

"Sorry, I can't. I already have plans. Maybe another time."

Erin smiled, "I'd like to say that I'm shocked, but I wanted to at least ask. So, you have a question for me?"

Nora stared at Toby. "I do. Any update from your colleague?"

"Not since we talked last. What's the rush?"

"The parents are having a hard time waiting."

"Well, I'll call if something breaks," Erin said. "I've got to run to a meeting. I'll talk to you later."

"Sure, okay."

After hanging up, she ran her hand over the smooth top of the crypod and peered in to the little boy — like she had at The Postponement Center for so many years. "Just a little while longer," she whispered.

After dressing herself and securing Toby under the lime blanket, Nora went to a credit union branch — a different location from the one visited during her lunch the day before. She knew of the governmental reporting required by the federal government with cash transactions over ten thousand dollars. Yesterday she withdrew nine thousand nine hundred dollars, but it probably wouldn't matter anyway as Nora planned to remain off the grid for a while.

She had removed all the money from her bedroom safe and taken advances on each of her credit cards. Not sure how much she would need, once found out, going into any financial institution or using plastic would be impossible. Nora knew her FICO score and credit absolutely would be ruined, she would sort that all out later. If there had only been more time to prepare.

She hoped the almost four hundred thousand dollars in her TPC 401k retirement plan would not be seized. Then again, she very well could be living off the Texas prison system soon.

Nora presented her driver's license to the service representative. "I would like to close my account."

"You've been a long-time member," said the polite woman. "Perhaps you'd like to keep your savings open?"

"No. I'm moving out of town."

The employee smiled. "Are you aware of our shared branching option? You can still be a member and do many of your same transactions through credit unions in your new city. Where are you going?"

Nora shifted in her seat. She didn't want to be in front of their security cameras any longer than she had to. "I just need to close the account and I'm in a hurry. How long will it take?"

The woman handed Nora a withdrawal slip to complete. "Shouldn't be long. I'm assuming you want this in a cashier's check?"

"No, cash."

"But —"

"Report it, if you must, but I'm requesting fifties and twenties."

The representative glanced around. "Are you under duress here, Ms. Collins?"

"I am not," responded Nora, forcing a smile. "I appreciate you asking."

She nodded and asked, "Forwarding address?"

"Not yet, I'll call and let you know," and she took one of the representatives business cards. There was no way she would be calling.

149

At the same moment Nora was leaving with money bundles tucked in the bottom of her purse, a couple walked hand-in-hand into the spacious lobby of The Postponement Center ready to meet their child for the first time. Excited, but with some trepidation, they approached a smiling receptionist.

"Good morning," said Christine.

"Good morning," replied the new father. "We are Ruben and Sylvia Martinez. We're here to pick up our son."

CHAPTER 35

Christine nodded and entered the couple's name on her computer. She frowned and tried again before looking up with a puzzled expression. "Scheduled for today?"

"Yes. I called your customer service people a few days ago," Sylvia said.

"I'm showing the reanimation as cancelled." The mother's jaw dropped.

"We did not cancel it," said Ruben.

The receptionist gave an unwavering smile motioning to the waiting area. "Why don't you go ahead and take a seat, Mr. and Mrs. Martinez, and I'll do some further checking. I just brewed a fresh pot of coffee, so please, help yourself."

As the Martinezes walked to the reception chairs, they whispered to each other. After out of ear shot, Christine tried a number, waited for several rings, but the call went straight to voice mail. She dialed another extension, "There's been some confusion on a client."

Ten minutes later, Marcia led the perplexed parents into the office of the CEO. "Please sit down, Dr. Thompson will be here momentarily. May I offer you some coffee or water?" They shook their heads and the administrative assistant exited closing the door.

Sylvia touched her stomach, unable to relax. "Something's wrong. I can feel it."

Ruben stared at the photograph of the doctor and his grandson hoping to soon possess a similar picture of himself and his own son. "I'm sure it's a mistake."

"No," she said, flatly, shaking her head.

Outside at Marcia's desk, Dr. Thompson stood behind her looking at her monitor. "Why would she rescind the request?"

Marcia shook her head, "Perhaps an error?"

"Nora doesn't make those kinds of mistakes. Find her and figure out what the hell she's doing. And find the neonate." He forced a smile while entering his office.

"Good morning. Pleasure seeing you again," he greeted them both with a handshake. He couldn't remember them specifically; he had performed so many postponement surgeries. Sitting down behind his desk, he folded his hands into a concerned doctor pose. "I understand you scheduled reanimation of your son for this morning."

The couple nodded as Dr. Thompson winced. "I'm embarrassed to say, he isn't quite ready to go, yet."

Ruben tilted his head, "Why not?"

"Unfortunately, we experienced a slight mix up with tracking." He wrinkled his forehead. "We have over twenty-seven hundred neonates in The Postponement Center system and occasionally communications get crossed. I do apologize."

Sylvia grimaced at her husband, "It was Nora's fault."

"She's trying to help," Ruben responded under his breath.

"She's pushy and I don't —"

"Excuse me?" interrupted Dr. Thompson.

Ruben sat back in his chair. "When can we pick him up?"

Following the head of TPC's cue, the Martinezes stood. "We will locate your son and give you a call surely within a couple of days. Again, please accept my apologies." They wanted to protest, however they were ushered to the door. "Don't worry, Mrs. Martinez. All will be fine. We'll contact you as soon as possible."

The parents had no other option or words to say. Ruben took hold of his wife's arm and they left. "Have a nice day, Mr. and Mrs. Martinez," Marcia called out. They did not respond. Once alone, she turned to the doctor standing in the doorway. "Amisha said she didn't show today. No message or email. She tried calling her at home and on her cell phone, but there was no answer. I couldn't reach her either."

Dr. Thompson put one hand on his hip and the other on his head. Another mess and it involved Nora.

CHAPTER 36

Michael wiped greasy hands on an already greasy rag and slammed the hood of an inconspicuous light blue 1970s Chevy pickup truck. Two years he'd spent in restoration and the only task remaining was the paint job. He couldn't decide candy apple red or a brighter glossy baby blue. He needed a color to garner some attention and maybe gain acceptance to one of Austin's classic car shows. Reaching up, he pulled down an oversized car cover and the edges dropped to the cement floor.

The overhead florescent lights gave everything a dull graininess. Tools, heavy totes and car parts crammed the space. From the back of a cupboard, he removed a bottle of rich amber colored Maker's 46 whiskey. After pouring himself a shot into a plastic cup, he perched himself on a wood stool at his workbench and taking out his phone he dialed.

The ringing cell made Nora jump as she sat on an unmade motel bed with her legs pulled up to her chest. She set the half-eaten protein bar down next to the balancing granny smith core on the bed stand, saw Michael's picture on her phone and answered. Staring at Toby's crypod, Nora tried hard to sound nonchalant. "Michael. Hey."

Surprised, he chided, "Wow, you're alive. Why don't you ever pick up or call me back?"

"Sorry. Been kind of busy."

"So. Designated as your 'Emergency Contact,' your work called looking for you."

She rubbed the pang in her gut. It had begun. "What did you say?"

"I told them I had no clue where you were."

"Good, keep it that way."

After a bit of awkward silence, he asked, "Well, where are you?" She did not respond. "Nora, what's going on?"

"I'll call you, but not for a while," she finally responded.

He stood sensing a seriousness in her voice. Something seemed wrong. "Are you in trouble? Should I be worried?"

"I love you, Michael," Nora said, then hung up.

Uncertain how to process such an unusual sentiment from his sister, he frowned and replied even though he knew the line was disconnected. "Um, I love you, too?"

CHAPTER 37

The next morning, Brady sat slumped at his workstation, JC propped himself up with extended arms. Dr. Thompson stood nearby, his hands shoved into the pockets of his lab coat. Behind them, Marcia leaned against the wall, her hand clapped over her mouth. All eyes were glued on two of the monitors as they watched a captured segment from the previous day's footage.

On one screen they saw Nora place a crypod unit into the back of her vehicle. Dr. Thompson folded his arms. He kicked himself for not letting Nora Collins go before any of this happened. There certainly had been plenty of opportunities to do so.

The second monitor showed Brady and JC in the employee break room heartily devouring sprinkle cupcakes and washing them down with coffee.

Brady scratched the back of his neck and JC's head fell into his palms. "We'll talk about this later, gentlemen," said the doctor in an exasperated tone as he strode from the security office with Marcia following close behind.

"Yes sir," responded the men in unison.

Brady pushed back in his chair, sullen-faced. JC paced from corner to corner in the small space, his face hot and stomach upset. How could he have been so stupid? In his twenty-two-year military career, he never endured such humiliation. He deserved any discipline Dr. Thompson might dish out for his inexcusable laziness and neglectfulness.

JC's anger with Nora's blatant betrayal was trumped by his own embarrassment of his lackadaisical attitude. He didn't want to lose his job. His years in the Marine Corps resulted in painful reminders with lingering back issues. After retiring, he had been grateful to find work with limited physical demands and few conflictual situations beyond an occasional frustrated parent. Despite the protesters walking in front of the campus, by law they were not permitted to step foot on private property. That had kept JC's position predictable and docile which was perfect for him.

CHAPTER 38

Two days later, as long as the couple could be put off, the Martinezes sat once again across from the TPC CEO. They were stiff and in shock. Ruben stared at the framed photograph and Sylvia's fingertips rested against her temples, suspecting Nora from the start. "I told you it was that woman."

Attempting to maintain control of the situation, Dr. Thompson kept his voice composed. "She removed him in his crypod, so I'm sure he's safe."

"How do you know?"

Ruben touched his wife's wrist, "Nora wouldn't hurt him."

Sylvia jerked her hand away. "She took him for herself."

The doctor reassured the parents, "That is not something Nora would do."

She leaned forward in her chair tapping her forefinger on the desk while she spoke. "She stood in my living room and told me I'd better wait to reanimate my son."

"Nora came to your home?" Dr. Thompson asked, knowing full well despite being against company policy, if anyone would break a rule, it would be Nora. Sylvia nodded. "Why did she try to convince you to leave him postponed?"

"Because he was born with a problem with his spine," answered Ruben, surprised. "Didn't you —"

"Yes, yes, I remember," Dr. Thompson said. The minor percentage of neonates with severe medical problems always proved touchy, but this case exceeded beyond any other.

Ruben continued, "She said we should wait for a full cure so —"

"I'm not waiting any longer," blurted out Sylvia getting to her feet. "We need to notify the police."

Dr. Thompson held his palms out trying to calm her. "Please, let's not over-react." Hiring a private investigator could save years of hellish public and legal repercussions because involving law enforcement surely would create an absolute PR nightmare for the organization and himself.

"Over-react?" Sylvia said, exasperated and infuriated with his lack of concern. "This is my child."

Dr. Thompson lowered his hands. "Of course, we are all concerned. But, let's not panic. Nora Collins is a trustworthy, long-term employee. Let me see if I can reason with her."

"You don't have any idea where she is," said Sylvia.

Both men rose and followed as she headed to the door. The doctor pleaded with the mother. "Please, Mrs. Martinez, give me a couple of days. I'm certain we can locate her and straighten everything out without causing any unwarranted alarm."

Turning back towards him, she jabbed an index finger into his chest. "You're more worried about your reputation then finding our child."

"No, that isn't —"

"We're going to the authorities," she said and stormed out of the office with her husband lagging behind.

Ruben looked back, "Please sir, try to find her...and my son." Then the couple was gone.

Dr. Thompson rubbed the nape of his neck muttering, "Damn it, Nora." He yelled for his assistant, "Marcia!"

A few seconds passed and she appeared in his office. "How'd it go?"

"Get Anderson on the phone." Marcia nodded and scurried off.

CHAPTER 39

Nora stood in front of a fully stocked selection of processed food snacks — chips, trail-mix, cookies, crackers, popcorn. She inspected the labels of some of the more tame looking treats, but found long lists of ingredients she struggled to recognize as healthy. Hydrogenated oil, polydextrose, vanillin, guar gum, sodium stearoyl lactylate, and what was yellow 6?

She wrinkled her nose at what so many people put in their bodies under the guise of food. The garbage receptacles by the soda machine were overflowing and the floors looked like they had not been mopped for weeks. Normally, Nora would not be caught dead in a corner convenience store, but until more time passed, this would have to do.

Settling on a small container of cottage cheese, some unsalted peanuts and a banana, she contemplated which water to buy.

A familiar and loud tone sounded in multiple locations. The cashier, a customer browsing the candy isle and Nora all glanced at their phones. An emergency message displayed on their screens:

AMBER ALERT
TRAVIS COUNTY, TX AMBER ALERT:
2011 SILVER HONDA CIVIC

As soon as Nora saw her license plate listed, her heart began racing. She placed the items on the nearest shelf and walked to the exit. The cashier eye-balled her like she might have stolen something, but, he did not chase her down.

She hurried to her car ignoring the homeless guy sleeping by the ice dispenser. Nora started her car, left the headlights off and drove around the store stopping in the alley.

Nora dug in one of the pockets in her backseat and found an old UT ball cap she had tucked away for no particular reason — at least not until now. All her hair was stuffed up into the hat and she sat for a few moments thinking, biting her lip and tapping on the steering wheel with her fingers.

The sudden ring of her phone caused her to jump, elevating her blood pressure even higher. The screen lit up her face in the dark interior as Dr. Thompson's name showed, again. She hit ignore and tried to calm herself down.

Not one to watch police shows on television, nor pay much attention to modern technology, aside from work stuff, she wondered if they might find her by tracking her cell. Just in case, Nora switched it off and attempted to remove the battery. Unable to open the casing, the only other thing to do was destroy the silly thing altogether. Better to not take a chance.

Nora got out and situated the slender communication device in front of her rear tire, then proceeded to drive back and forth until it lie in pieces. From there she tossed the smashed remains into the nearby dumpster. Mission accomplished. Now for the next challenge.

An idea popped into her head and she pulled away turning on her headlights only after she was out of the alley. Nora stayed on back roads until she reached a modest brick house set to one side of a three acre plot. Once again, she turned the lights off until passing the home. Due to the late hour, only a single light glowed inside the house. The car moved so slow, she could get out and crawl faster.

The driveway ended after twenty yards. A gravel road continued for another ten. At the end was a free-standing double garage, one Nora hadn't been in for many months, perhaps a couple of years.

The barn styled doors opened with little effort and only a faint creak. Using a flashlight kept in her glovebox, she walked to the workbench. "Please be there," she murmured to herself. Inside one of the upper cupboards, the beam shined upon two sets of keys hanging on a hook. A little smile came to Nora's face.

She removed the cover from Michael's blue Chevy pickup. Her brother had done a nice restoration job and she hoped he had put the engine back in. The current Texas plates seemed encouraging, but gave no guarantee.

She climbed in the driver's seat and sat for a moment. One of three things would happen next. First, the truck may not start and she had no plan B. Second, the truck would start and be one of those obnoxious deafening engines rumbling everyone awake inside the house. Or third, the truck would start and run flawless.

Holding her breath, she slipped the key into the ignition and turned it. She exhaled as the third alternative came true.

After pulling out of the garage, she backed in her car placing her keys on the front driver's seat.

The car cover didn't fit right, but she pulled it over the Honda, regardless. She swung the doors closed and left in Michael's truck.

Forty-five minutes later at the open door of the motel room, Nora scanned for anything forgotten. The full backpack dangled over her shoulder as she extinguished the light and clicked the door shut.

Nora put her hand on the crypod sitting on the front seat and whispered, "Don't worry, Toby. All is well." Then she secured the unit and covered it with the green blanket, muting out the soft blue illumination.

CHAPTER 40

The housekeeper went about her daily routine of replacing the worn towels and changing the sheets. She poured bowl cleaner in the toilet and swirled around a brush. Some stray hairs disappeared down the drain when she rinsed the sink. Sliding back the shower curtain, she determined it didn't look bad and she could clean that next time.

The woman checked the trash cans since sometimes people threw away interesting things. She fished out the odd square object having not seen anything like it before. Thinking it might be something, she put the heavy black item on top of her supply cart.

Several hours later, the housekeeper approached the motel lobby and waited for the day clerk to come out from the back room.

"Hola," she said, dumping her findings from the day on the counter: one gold hoop earring, a wadded up blue T-shirt, and the black cube. He picked up the battery and turned it over in his hand. "Worth any dollars?" she asked.

The clerk examined all sides and on the bottom he noticed the TPC company logo. "Maybe."

CHAPTER 41

JC shifted from one foot to the other and back again as he observed the gathering crowd in front of The Postponement Center. For the designated twenty minute press conference, additional security guards had been hired and they stood on the outskirts of the attendees.

Media crews readied by testing microphones, checking camera settings and moving as far forward as they could gaining prime spots. Parents with clutched hands rose on tip-toes trying to see. Regular TPC protesters buzzed about being allowed to step on company property legally for the first time after having agreed to play nice and not chant.

Upon the suggestion of TPC's public relations head, who had consulted via phone due to being out of the country, Dr. Thompson had arrived early and parked his sleek ebony Porsche 911 in the back of the building out of view from anyone's critical eye. He walked up to Marcia and TPC counsel, Doug Anderson, waiting inside the protected confines of the locked lobby.

Marcia handed him prepared statements. "With the revisions."

"Thanks," Dr. Thompson said without taking his eyes off the growing swarm outside.

"You should have fired that damn woman a long time ago," said the lawyer.

The CEO tugged on his coat. "You really think this jacket is necessary? It seems a bit pretentious and the humidity is sweltering."

Anderson ignored the concerns and offered final instructions. "Stay on topic like we discussed. Don't allow yourself to be sucked into a moral debate."

Dr. Thompson referred to a wall clock. Eleven straight up. He inhaled a slow breath and exhaled it.

"Just keep focused," said Doug. "You had better quell the fear of those parents otherwise you're going to be dealing with a shit load of lawsuits."

Christine and Amisha stood behind the reception desk staring at their boss as he pushed the door open and exited. The attorney followed. When he approached the podium, the buzzing parents, protesters and reporters began to quiet down.

"Good morning. Thank you for coming. My name is Dr. Leonard Thompson, Senior Obstecryogenist and CEO for The Postponement Center. Our primary goal here is to provide service to our community. We care about the parents we serve and their children."

Dr. Thompson set his notes down before he dropped them and continued, "TPC is active in several local children's charities, and educational programs. We ensure the non-profit *Saved By Postponement* organization is adequately funded so they may offer needed services for those less fortunate."

An anti-postponement protester yelled out, "It's unethical to put off a life for convenience."

Thompson disregarded the lonely comment as security approached the protester. "TPC has been recognized as a model corporate citizen and our employees volunteer hundreds of hours in this community."

Christine looked at Amisha. "We haven't given one hour to charity since that wine-tasting fundraiser Nora planned three years ago." Amisha grimaced.

"Are all the children safe?" came a question from the audience.

"Yeah, is my kid okay?" asked a worried father.

"This is a unique case. The infants are safe and there are no risks."

"Then why can't I get her?" the father said.

The doctor leaned closer to the microphone. "We house many neo — babies here," he caught himself, remembering he was not supposed to use the term neonates; it was too clinical sounding. "Our excellent staff are handling reanimations as quickly as possible. Procedures and paperwork take time and we can only do so much. Many parents continue to request postponements."

"Which is exactly what started this whole mess," hollered Jillian, the red head, "Parents who don't care!" JC glanced over seeing the pushy leader and young Emma standing by her side. He nodded toward security to get closer to these two in case of another outbreak.

Several disgruntled people groaned and responded. "That's none of your business. You don't know what you're talking about."

Emma found herself feeling warm, rolled up the sleeves of her blouse, and managed to call out, "What's being done to find the missing baby?"

Appreciative for a more benign question, Dr. Thompson answered. "We're doing everything feasible to locate the Martinez child including working closely with authorities and the —"

"Is it true that the child has a medical issue?" someone shouted.

"We are not at liberty to share that information."

Doug Anderson crossed his arms sensing the crowd's anxiety rising.

"Postponement should be banned. Who cares about convenience, they are humans," screamed a protester.

Some of the parents began to argue with the demonstrators around them returning bold claims, anger in their voices. "We've got the right to decide," and "You have no grounds to tell us what to do."

Jillian reveled in her sly, poignant pot-stirring. She pointed at the TPC CEO, company counsel, and those recognizable proponents of legalized postponement. "All you people will burn in hell."

Emma turned and stared at Jillian.

Acknowledging the confusion in Emma's eyes, Jillian took a hold of her arm. "This is how we make change, hon. Don't feel bad," she consoled rubbing her shoulder. "These people create their own messes. They're simply not mature enough to deal with the outcome."

"I thought we were here for the babies?"

"Oh Emma, it all starts when these types of women are so promiscuous." She smiled and winked showing no regard as to the efficacy of her statement. "Come on, things are just getting fun."

Emma slammed her picket sign hard into Jillian's chest and walked away pushing through the jam-packed people. Jillian shook her head then returned her attention to the side-stepping occurring at the front.

Anderson frowned at Dr. Thompson indicating not to swallow the bait. His client took in a fast, deep breath and raised his palms trying to settle the people. "Please, let's remain focused on why we are here."

"Where is Nora Collins?" A father called out, "Why can't you find her?"

Another woman fighting off tears, blurted, "You obviously can't protect the children entrusted to you."

"I told you, all the neonates are fine," Dr. Thompson said, realizing he had allowed that forbidden word to slip from his lips.

"Tell that to the Martinezes," mocked Jillian. She bobbed her head up and down thinking that had been quite the zinger.

Dr. Thompson tightened his jaw knowing he was getting drawn in. "Postponement practices save lives and makes for healthier children." Anderson took in the mass of people who were becoming more agitated, yelling out accusations and threats at each other. He decided it had been erroneous to include the public and those activists.

"It's a profit making scheme," one of the new demonstrators called.

Jillian nodded in approval and added, "The money from postponing babies is going right into your pocket."

Dr. Thompson bristled, "We are a heavily regulated industry providing legal services to women and —"

"What's your salary? Do you make bonuses, Dr. Thompson?" Jillian said. All grew silent. "You have a big house? A corporate jet? Private schools for your kids? Admit it, Doctor, you're making bank at the expense of children."

The security guards and police officers straightened up, preparing to intervene as the people started inching forward. Dr. Thompson's patience had all but expired and beads of perspiration dripped from his face. "It offers a viable alternative for —"

Anderson stepped to the mic shoving the doctor aside. He must regain some control before a riot broke and he spoke in a loud, authoritative voice. "Cryonics is a legal and private affair for parents."

The amplified voice of the TPC attorney echoed off the exterior glass wall. "Our clients reserve the right to choose a postponement option for whatever reason they determine to be best for themselves and their offspring."

From the mouth of Jillian tumbled another inciting declaration, "Your only interest is profits on the backs of innocent children."

With clenched fists, a father standing next to her turned. "Why don't you shut up! You don't know what the hell you're talking about."

"Of course I do." she said, taunting. "You're just not capable enough to handle the consequences of what's in your pants." The guy's wife fought to keep her husband from going after Jillian.

"Please, calm down," came Anderson's booming voice creating screeching feedback from the speakers. But the crowd, now turning gang-like, had passed beyond peaceful as emotions swelled.

"Let the babies live. Let the babies live," roared one protester. Others soon joined in the chant, egging on the parents who started to shove the protesters backwards.

The surrounding officers drew nearer attempting to break up the angry mob. Reporters enjoyed the excitement as cameras and cell phones captured images and words already being shared on social media and across news outlets.

The lawyer moved away from the podium as JC hurried him and Dr. Thompson towards the building entrance.

From her car, Emma watched and listened to the noise of unrest through her open windows. Her folks had encouraged her to stop being so shy and reserved; to come out of her shell. To assist their daughter in developing her confidence and assertiveness skills, they had enlisted a long-time friend and activist to help. Jillian promised Emma's mother and father that she would mentor their youngest and show her how to fight for a cause, how to take a stand, how to be an adult.

Emma wanted to get involved, but regardless of what her parents thought, harassment and intimidation was not what she wished to engage in. No matter how much she disagreed with the postponement choice, treating people with such hate and contempt seemed over-zealous and plain wrong. Jillian's unfair sweeping generalizations, made Emma nauseas. Things do happen sometimes.

Nora stood to switch off the motel television. She checked into this hotel without a hitch a few hours before. Walking over to Toby, she placed her hand on the cool Plexiglass and peered at the motionless outline within the white mist. Leaning down, she kissed the top of the crypod, just six inches above the sweet face of the slumbering boy for whom she would do anything to protect. "I'll be back soon."

CHAPTER 42

A Breakfast Bite Cafe customer raised his arm. "I'll take the check." Ruben nodded and went to the computer to ring in the final charges.

The hostess approached and slipped him a folded over note. "Tessa found this on one of the back tables with your name on it." She hurried away to greet newly arrived patrons.

The jagged paper with his name written on it was torn from the cafe's menu. He unfolded it blinking several times at the scribbled handwriting. Upon seeing the words HE IS SAFE, Ruben charged across the restaurant to the back section. A woman occupied the booth where he and Nora had spoken weeks earlier. Could it be her? Unable to tell from behind, he ran to her almost knocking down another server.

When he reached the table, she smiled up at him. "Can I order an egg and cheese croissant and some sweet tea?"

Ruben bolted for the door pushing past surprised customers waiting in line to be seated. The manager watched him as he dashed out of the front entrance and stood on the sidewalk under a Texas summer downpour. Desperate to see Nora, his head moved in all directions, but she was gone.

During the remainder of his shift, Ruben mulled over if he should tell Sylvia about the message or not. Their child was not in danger and his wife deserved to know. However, he also knew she wouldn't be so forgiving. He trusted Nora and always had, for some reason. She seemed to have uncommon concerns about his son, although he never expected her to go to such extremes. If he just could have convinced Sylvia to wait.

A squad car sat parked by their house when he got home that afternoon. That happened on a regular basis now so he no longer worried when he saw one.

Sylvia carried two glasses towards the living room when she spotted her husband standing in the entryway, pondering. "I didn't hear you come in," she said.

"Anything going on?" he asked.

"They think she's still in town. I guess somebody found a crypod battery."

Ruben did not react nor make eye-contact. "What's wrong?" He bit his lip and stared at the floor. Sylvia set the water on a side table and placed her hands on her husband's arms. "Rube, what's going on? Are you sick?"

After some hesitation, he withdrew the note from his pocket and handed it to her. "He is safe," she read out loud as she felt her heart begin to speed up. "Where did you get this? Did you talk to her?"

"Shh," he said attempting to keep their conversation private. "She left it at the cafe. I tried to find her, but —"

Sylvia turned intending to deliver the new evidence to the men awaiting her return, but Ruben grabbed her arm, raising his voice. "No!" he exclaimed more forceful. "Maybe we should wait."

"What? Why?

"Because I think she's trying to help," he said.

Her head pulled back in surprise. "You still trust her after she took our son?"

"I can't believe she —"

Sylvia cut him off. "She has no children. She isn't married. And now they say she had this strange attraction to all those babies." Ruben didn't respond. "She wanted a child so she took ours. Nora Collins took our baby!"

He shook his head, "That's silly, she wouldn't do that."

Sylvia rolled her eyes. "Our boy is growing up in someone else's arms."

"He's not awake, I know."

"How do you know? She didn't say that in this," she waved the paper in front of his face.

A police officer popped his head around the corner. "Everything alright?"

The Martinezes stared at each other. Though his eyes pleaded with her not to tell, she paused. Then turned to the officer and held out the paper.

CHAPTER 43

It had been a long few weeks for JC. Since the press conference, the protesters became more brazen trying to inch themselves further on the property. He pushed them back almost every day. Most of the time the threat of calling the police worked in getting them to retreat the thirty yards back to the sidewalk.

After parking in his driveway, he grabbed his lunch bag and John Grisham novel, and headed to the front door. Gertie, his adopted terrier-mix, began barking inside the house knowing her master had arrived.

As he reached for the handle, he stopped. "JC," came a woman's voice again from the side of the house and he dropped the items in his hand on the porch seat and went to investigate.

Walking towards the call, Nora stepped out from behind the mature Rose of Sharon bushes. Despite the stifling humid weather, she wore a black sweatshirt with the hood up.

"Nora?" He was shocked by her presence.

"Hey JC."

"What the hell are you doing here?" he said, coming closer. "What are you doing at all? Do you have a clue about how much chaos you have caused? And how do you know where I live?"

Nora glanced down and touched one of the large pink blooms, "I followed you home, yesterday."

JC surveyed his middle-class neighborhood, but no one seemed to notice the kidnapper standing in front of him. The widowed father across the street struggled to buckle his two young children in the minivan. "I pegged you as one of the good ones," JC said, returning his attention to Nora.

He knew his comment hurt when she swallowed a lump away in her throat. "I am," she tried to sound convincing to both of them. She attempted to lighten the mood. "Gave you a little excitement, huh?"

But he did not flinch, instead he shoved his hands into his uniform pants pockets. "That is an understatement. You got Brady and me into serious trouble. Do you realize how humiliating that was? You took advantage of us, made us appear foolish."

"I'm sorry."

The elderly man next door parted his curtains and gave a friendly wave. JC waved back and the drapes shut again. Gertie began whimpering and scratching at the door.

"How is Brady?" Nora asked.

"Thompson forced him into retirement. I don't understand why you did it. What were you thinking? If you wanted one so bad, why didn't you just adopt like other people do."

"I didn't do it to keep him. Is that what you believe?"

He shrugged, not buying it. "What other explanation could there be?"

"Not that one," she said then wiped perspiration from her forehead. "There wasn't another option."

He awaited a more logical reason but Nora decided to go right to why she had taken a chance coming to him. "JC, I need your help with a few more supplies."

His face balled up. "What? You've managed to get me in enough hot water."

"I know, I apologize." Nora offered a slight smile, "How were the cupcakes?"

"Pretty damn tasty," he replied, exhaling some tension. "But, I can't be a part of this."

"No one will find out. It would only be a couple batteries, it will go unnoticed if you take them from the —"

"No, I will not become involved," he said with a steadfast resolution. Then added a softer apology, "Sorry."

She sighed and bit her lower lip. "Maybe Christine would help?"

"Listen Nora. A lot of people are upset about what you did. No one's going to help you. Parents are threatening to sue and now those demonstrators have even more fuel for their cause. It's been awful around there. You need to just return the kid."

She shook her head. "You don't understand. I'm only —"

"Please, don't tell me," JC said lifting his open palms. "This job is important to me and I can't afford to lose it. My wife isn't working and our oldest is starting college in the fall."

"If you could just —"

"Honestly, I should turn you in." Her eyes cast to the ground. "Yet, I always liked you. Everyone wants you to bring the baby back." Nora didn't respond. JC saw the ASU logo on her sweatshirt. "You went to Arizona State? My brother attended for three years."

Gertie's barking borderlined frenzy as the deadbolt unlocked and the door opened. "JC?" his wife called out. Nora jumped back behind the foliage. "The dog's going crazy. Is everything okay?"

Like a bullet, the wiry-haired pooch escaped and bolted straight to where Nora stood hiding. She held her breath. At the last moment, the TPC security guard scooped the squirming animal up into his arms and kissed his wife. "Yup, everything's fine." He placed his hand on the small of her back and ushered her back inside the house, following behind. Right before he closed the door, he looked to see Nora walking at a fast clip down the street with her head down.

CHAPTER 44

Erin carried her sleeping daughter into her bedroom. Kayla's relaxed body tumbled easily to the bed and her mother pulled off her bright pink boots topped with soft white faux fur. It didn't matter that it was almost one hundred degrees with unbearable humidity, Kayla insisted on wearing her favorite gift from last Christmas. However, as fast as she was growing, they would be too tight within the next month. Erin smiled as she watched her little girl slumbering so sound. She brushed the dirty blonde hair back from her daughter's face and covered her with a beloved Cinderella comforter.

Leaving Kayla's door part-way open, she went to the garage and reemerged carrying canvas grocery bags over both shoulders and a Whole Foods paper sack. She switched on the six o'clock news to catch up on the world. Between twelve-hour work days, and her daughter, that didn't leave much time left. Fruits, vegetables, canned goods and fresh salmon began finding their proper homes.

Erin didn't pay much attention to the local commercials and disappeared into her over-sized walk-in pantry putting groceries away. While unpacking she heard a voice, "It's a heart-wrenching story, the child missing for two weeks. Yet, Ruben and Sylvia Martinez have not given up hope."

Erin stopped and looked at the television. Abductions were horrible and she couldn't imagine how terrifying it would be for a mother.

A reporter stood next to the parents. "The woman that authorities are searching for works at an organization where the controversial newborn postponement services are conducted. The boy was in a postponed state when this woman, Nora Collins, allegedly took him." Nora's employee picture from TPC filled the screen.

With an arm full of organic carrots, their cool green tops laying across her forearms, Erin's mouth opened, dumbfounded as she stared at the photograph. "Holy shit."

"The Martinezes are anxious to find their infant," said the reporter.

Sylvia leaned forward. "If anyone knows where our baby is or where Nora Collins is, please call the police. We will do anything to bring our son home. We just...just..." She broke into tears, her exterior resilience crumbling. Ruben put his arm around his exhausted wife.

The reporter said, "If you have any information, contact the..."

Erin grabbed her cell from her purse and dialed Nora's number. Why would she have done this? Taken someone else's child. The phone did not ring at all, instead a recorded message played. "This mailbox is full. Try your call again later."

Back on the news, Ruben pulled the microphone to himself and peered into the camera. "Please Nora. Bring Toby home."

Nora witnessed Ruben's plea while standing in front of the TV in her latest motel room. She muted the volume and thought for thirty seconds. Dressed in old running clothes, she donned a baseball cap, covering her graying roots, and slipped on dark glasses.

She began her daily exercise to burn off tension built up by her self-imposed prison, even if for a short period. Living standards had dropped significantly with the need to use cash in lieu of a license and credit card. The rooms defined sleazy, rented more by the hour than the night. But most people stuck to themselves, in all likelihood due to questionable covert activities — although, she doubted any of them would be in possession of a stolen baby. Of course, Nora knew her true intentions for Toby. All her actions focused on ensuring him a better life. No one could understand, especially not his mother.

During the run, her mind returned to TPC. She had not anticipated feeling nostalgic for the job routine and wondering about the babies. Never wanting a single one of those special lives to feel lonely or abandoned, Nora had remained convinced that the children sensed when people came near. Aside from machine maintenance, nobody else paid any attention to them.

The littered rundown park, similar to the neighborhood surrounding the motel, didn't stop the patrons from coming. She slowed to a walk and used her shirt to wipe sweat from her sunglasses. A small playground held almost a dozen occupied children. Two boys hung upside down by their legs from the monkey bars. Others rocked with wild motion while clinging to fading plastic roosters or horses secured to the sand with oversized springs. A group laughed nonstop as they chased each other shooting water from neon orange and yellow squirt guns.

Some children beckoned their parents to watch them on the slide, come push them on the swing, see what they could do. The adults waved and kept texting; smiled and continued gossiping; ignored their offspring, preoccupied with their own private distractions.

CHAPTER 45

The florescent light over Michael's workbench flickered on. Normally dedicated at getting out to his "man-cave," as Bree called it, at least four or five times a month, life had gotten in the way the past several weeks. That night she pushed him out the back door saying it would be healthy for him to take time for himself — to rejuvenate his spiritual something or other.

In reality, the break sounded perfect; a chance to clear his mind from accelerated depreciation schedules and liquidity ratios. But more important was avoiding the weekly television show on angel-beings that his girlfriend refused to skip. She drove hard to convince him of all the evidence that they walked among us. In fact, she swore her co-worker was one of these special people.

With the on-boarding of new accounting clients, things were hectic at work requiring an exorbitant amount of overtime. On the home-front, getting his boys packed and ready for summer camp proved a feat in itself. And, of course, dealing with seeing his sister's photograph plastered all over the media like a wanted criminal brought a lot of questions.

When Nora's boss called saying she kidnapped a neonate, Michael figured it ridiculous. "We've got her on the surveillance cameras," Dr. Thompson claimed.

"There must have been a good reason," Michael said, not liking the accusation.

"Mr. Collins, there is no acceptable explanation for the actions of your sister." Nora's brother did not respond. "Let us know if she contacts you."

"Right," he said, knowing he would never do such a thing. The police visited a couple of times, but he had nothing to help them.

Michael opened a wood storage cabinet — one he built and refinished himself almost a decade ago. Reaching to the far back, he retrieved his prize. The contents in the bottle of Maker's 46 poured easily into a cup and more easily down his throat. After a few swigs of whiskey, he felt Bree may have been right, his spirit was rejuvenating...something.

Nora entered his rambling thoughts. She struggled to fit in with employees at all her jobs and didn't handle things in the most rational manner sometimes. Even as a child, but more so after quitting college, her way of working through conflict consisted of denying it, ignoring it, and then abandoning it.

For many years Michael resented his sister for ducking out of those challenging years with their aging parents. Yet, as time went on, he came to accept that she simply could not deal with the demands and stress. What was he to do? She was his sister, no matter how irresponsible she had been. And, who knew what Nora was up to now? Michael honestly could not fathom her kidnapping a baby. It just made no sense.

Anxious to finish the final step on the rebuilt Chevy and move on to the next project, he thumbed through paint samples. Obtaining that Mustang promised to keep him distracted for a while. Yet the decision on the truck color had to come first.

Michael glanced over to the vehicle draped by the car cover. Within one second he realized something was not right and he rose from his stool and yanked the canvas back part way revealing

Nora's Civic. "What the —" He put the butt of his hand against his forehead. "What did she do?"

Through the window, he saw her set of keys on the front seat. Michael rubbed his chin, turned in a circle a few times and kept staring at her car. "Nora, you're in deep shit," he muttered. Then it hit him that he might be in trouble as well. How dare she involve him! He had a life and a family.

After some choice words, he pulled the cover back over the Honda. Michael finished his drink while allowing the realization that now he was illegally protecting Nora sink in. He turned off the light, closed the garage doors and returned to his house.

CHAPTER 46

Erin stood at a counter covered with research testing equipment — microscopes, centrifuges, and many varied screens. She wore a white lab coat and typed at a rapid pace at a computer.

Her cell phone rang and she answered while placing her hands back on the keyboard and continuing to type, her eyes focused on the monitor. "This is Erin."

"Erin, it's —"

"Nora?" she broke in, recognizing her voice immediately. "Where are you?"

Nora stood outside a convenience store talking on a pay phone holding the receiver with several Subway napkins being sure it did not touch her face. "I can't say."

Erin walked from her work area into the hallway concerned others might hear the conversation. "You're all over the news."

"I know," said Nora. "What's the status of the research?"

The realization hit her like a ton of bricks. "Oh Nora, this is the sick baby? You kidnapped that couple's sick baby?"

A long pause permeated the air before confirmation came. "Yes. But, I didn't kidnap him."

"The hell you didn't," said Erin, her voice filled with accusation.

"Look, it's just for a little while until you guys find the full cure."

Erin shook her head knowing this made no sense. "You can't do it this way. If you get caught, you're going to jail." Nora remained silent. "Please, bring him back now."

"I can't do that, not yet. The timing isn't right."

No doubt in her mind that the situation could not end well, Erin softened her tone hoping to talk some sense into her friend. "Where are you? I'm worried about you."

Nora ignored the sympathy for her own well-being, Toby being the primary concern. "How much longer on the treatment?"

Erin sighed, "You're not thinking right, you —"

Unable to stop from raising her voice, Nora repeated her question. "How much longer?"

"Too long to keep running."

"I'll check back."

"Please, you aren't his mother. You shouldn't be the one making this decision."

"Of course, I'm not his mother. This isn't about me."

"Oh, it isn't?"

Nora hung up. Her heart pounded with agitation.

She may not be Toby's mother, yet the outcome would prove best for all — except herself. She spent more time with Toby than anyone else, even his own parents. As one of the first babies postponed for medical reasons, Nora had visited him, talked to him, and taken care of him almost daily for the past seven years. She refused to give up. Everyone claimed her as the bad person, but she would suffer the most.

CHAPTER 47

Nora dumped nasty black liquid in the sink, watched the swirling and disappearance down the drain. Her nostrils filled with the ugly odor of terrible, cheap coffee. Knowing she should be grateful for having a pot and packaged grounds at all, that day it simply disgusted her. She decided to walk down to a local place spotted when arriving at her latest place of residence.

To help blend in better, she recently bought a blonde wig. The synthetic strands came to her shoulders and she shoved her own light brown hair up into the cap. Adjusting the volume on the television to a moderate level, she draped the lime green blanket over the crypod, and placed her duffle bag on top. Not that those precautions would stop anyone from finding the unit, but perhaps Toby might go unnoticed if someone came in the room. Her sunglasses went on and the do-not-disturb sign was looped around the door handle.

Warm temperatures and sticky humidity had not yet disappeared in Austin despite being late September and Nora worked up a sweat walking along the street. That hairpiece irritated her head. It was hot and itchy and she scratched her scalp beneath the snug band.

The small coffee shop felt claustrophobic with only ten customers and while she waited, two more women entered and got in line behind her. Through her peripheral vision, Nora saw one wore a shiny grape-colored top with a crocheted neckline and the other squeezed into skin-tight tangerine pants. They talked non-stop and refused to take Nora's polite side-steps to the left indicating they were invading her private space. They jabbered on about so-and-so's marriage, last weekend's party disaster, and their husband's narcissistic behavior.

Upon reaching the front counter, Nora put in her order, not removing the dark glasses.

"You got it. A large iced coffee," said the young man raising a pen to the empty cup. "And your name?"

She didn't expect the innocent question. "Uh, Nancy."

"Be right up, Nancy," responded the cashier.

Nora nodded and stood by the delivery station still hearing the gossips. Once collecting her drink, she chose a small table in the back, enjoying her few minutes out of the motel. The coffee tasted bold and rich, a little like heaven after what she had been ingesting. Even though she considered herself to be naturally introverted, after having minimal interaction for three months, she experienced a strange welcomed pleasure being around other people.

The two ladies selected a table near Nora. As they sat down, they gave her a sideways glance. Tangerine pants wouldn't be caught dead associating with a woman dressed like that and whispered to her friend, "Can't even. Someone purchased an outfit at Goodwill." Which of course, was true. Nora shopped there the previous week hoping to add some new additions to her lackluster wardrobe.

"This neighborhood has really declined," said tangerine pants.

"Yeah. I hardly ever come here anymore," agreed grape top. "I just love those shoes. Are they new?" Tangerine pants bragged about how she always found the best shoe deals.

For the next few minutes Nora could not avoid listening to the two friends continue on about mineral-based makeup, the aluminum in antiperspirant, and the fall sale at Macy's.

Ugh, Nora thought to herself. *Is this what the real world's like?* Everything seemed so mundane and petty compared to what she was doing, living on the fringe. She took another sip of coffee. Then the conversation took a more personal turn.

"Didn't your sister have a baby at that Postponement place?" asked tangerine pants.

"Yes, but she got him out before all this fiasco began," grape top said. "It's awful what that woman did, kidnapping a child because she couldn't have one herself."

Tangerine pants shook her head. "I guess she couldn't find a man to sleep with her. Did you see how frumpy she was?" The women cackled. "And old. Lord, can you imagine —"

But before she finished, Nora rose to her feet and mysteriously stumbled spilling the remainder of her iced drink all over tangerine pants' new shoes.

"What the f —"

"Oh, I'm so sorry about that," Nora interrupted with a fake sincere tone. The woman swore like a drunken sailor, grabbing the single napkin Nora held out in her hand and attempting to wipe away the liquid-stains.

"Do you know how much —" started the angry woman but the culprit had already slipped out of the shop.

With a satisfied smirk on her face, Nora strode down the street. She had got even, ruining those horrid shoes. After walking for a minute, her smile faded as she tried not to let those women's comments penetrate her feelings.

A pumping rap song rattled Nora's insides as a cobalt blue low-rider Chevy Impala cruised up next to her. She glanced over and a guy in his mid-twenties hung out of the passenger window.

"Hey niña, wanna ride?" Then the driver engaged the hydraulics causing the car to start bouncing.

Nora jumped, her heart thumping as loud as the bass notes in the music. The young men laughed as they passed by leaving her breathless. She needed to get back to her room. Back to safety and calm. Back with Toby.

CHAPTER 48

A refreshing morning breeze blew through the open window at Nora's latest hideout. At last, the drop in temperatures had brought about leaves of bright yellows and tarnished reds.

Boredom took over most days. Nora flipped from channel to channel: soap operas, product promotions, old movies. It didn't matter much as long as her mind stayed occupied. Yesterday had been shower day. Since she hadn't been running, there didn't seem to be a need to do it daily anymore.

So far, she liked that location. The staff did not appear nosy and the end room provided relative quiet most times. But another move was overdue. Afraid to stay longer than ten days in each place, her time there had exceeded two weeks.

Another moving day, Nora thought while beginning to gather items together. She put a new, well new to her, pair of running shoes discovered at Goodwill a month earlier and dropped them into her bag wondering if she'd ever go back to using them.

Nora's attention caught on a home-grown commercial. Batteries 4 You guaranteed to carry or obtain any battery needed by their customers. An issue percolated. The final two batteries she continued switching held less of a charge now. Nora considered the risk of a visit to the specialty store. Yet, the consequences of not doing so seemed worse.

She removed the half-charged one from the recharger and examined it. The Postponement Center logo on the base would be a dead giveaway. With a permanent black marker from the bottom of a bag pocket, she marked through the identifying lettering as best she could and slipped the heavy square into an oversized brown purse — another second-hand find.

The retailer was only a short ride away. To remain as low-key as possible, Nora always went on foot or took public transportation to places, keeping Michael's pickup truck in the most inconspicuous spot in the parking lot. Nora performed the normal preparation ritual before she left the room: television audible, blanket and duffle atop the crypod, baseball cap over the blonde hairpiece, black ASU sweatshirt and sunglasses on, and do-not-disturb sign hanging from the door knob.

With bus routes second nature, she hopped on one that released her across the street from Batteries 4 You. She drew in a deep breath expecting surveillance monitoring, yet Nora hoped law enforcement had not notified such retailers about the article she sought. Since most media outlets assumed she reanimated Toby for herself, and, as of late, dirty senate politics and a recent car-jacking spree consumed the Austin news programs, Nora had a chance.

The door opened and an unusual, metallic-type odor filled her nostrils. The well-stocked shelves displayed batteries of every shape and size imaginable. A guy in his early twenties stood behind a display case talking on the phone.

She wandered around hoping to locate what she was hunting for, but no such luck. The clerk completed his call, then approached. "Can I help you find something?"

Here we go, thought Nora turning to greet the young man. She pulled the black battery out and held it up. "Yes, I'm looking for something like this."

He took the object from her and rotated it in his hands. "Huh." His furrowed brow indicated some confusion. "What's this for?"

She had prepared for this question. "It's for my dad. For an old wheelchair, I think."

"Let me see," the clerk said, walking back to the front desk to begin his computer investigation. After a minute of dead ends, he said, "Hold on," and disappeared into the back room.

Nora folded her arms across her chest. Behind the false protection of her sunglasses, she moved her eyes to the upper corners of each wall. Four security cameras blinked red lights and she acted nonchalant by perusing a flashlight rack.

Ten long excruciating minutes passed before the clerk re-emerged from the back room followed by an older gentleman, likely the boss. "Where exactly did you get this?" asked the manager holding the battery in his hand, the name, Zach, on his tag.

Butterflies flew in every which direction in Nora's stomach. "My dad. He picked it up at a garage sale or something." She forced a smile. "He likes discovering weird old stuff."

"I don't think it is very old." He turned it over pointing at the black marks. "Somebody's crossed through the manufacturer name."

She glanced down, "Oh, I see," she said, feigning surprise.

"We've checked our extensive database and found nothing matching for consumer use."

Uneasiness grew as she recovered the battery from Zach who was slow to relinquish it. "Okay, I'll let him know."

"Although, we did find that this type is manufactured specifically for businesses involved with cryonics. For those machines where they keep things frozen."

"Wow, really?" Nora tucked the precious item back inside her purse. "Dad sure made a find this time," she joked. The clerk and manager stared at her. "Well, I appreciate you checking."

"No problem," called out the younger man with enthusiasm as she went for the door. "Normally we can find anything. Come back again."

Nora walked at a brisk pace, fighting the temptation to look back. She rounded the first corner, and a second. A black and white police car headed down the street towards her and she ducked through the closest graffitied door and stood gazing back through a Windex-streaked window. The squad car drove by and she began breathing again.

"What can I getcha?" boomed a deep voice. Her head snapped to the face of a heavy-set, bearded man with colorful neck tattoos.

"Uh," she stammered.

"Got a new local IPA on special."

Unable to process anything more complicated, Nora said, "Fine." He nodded and walked away as she cozied up to the sticky wooden surface. She mopped the sweat from her forehead on a white cocktail napkin before dropping her trembling hands to her lap.

Soon he returned with a tall amber glass of beer. "Starting a tab?" The bar smelled rank. The only other customer at the far end of the counter stood and extended her arms to steady her balance while she conquered the fifteen steps to the restroom.

Nora handed a ten dollar bill to the bartender. "No thanks. Keep the change." He acknowledged the generous tip and left her alone.

If the Zach guy reported his suspicions to the authorities, then she showed up in some other retailer — that would be her end! She expelled the thought from her head about what could happen to Toby if she did not return to him in time, or at all. She sipped her brew, recoiling, having never tasted such a strong and bitter flavor.

The drunk woman arrived unannounced and unexpected when she plunked down on the neighboring stool. Nora combed through her bag pretending to search for something. *Why did she come over here?*

"Do I know you?" the woman asked. "It seems like I should."

"No," said Nora without looking up.

"You look so familiar," she persisted, her eyes squinting in an attempt to focus. She called out, a definite slur in her voice. "Another round. Like one for both of us."

"Thank you, but I'm leaving," said Nora, standing and thinking she should have gone back to the motel right away.

The woman placed her hand on Nora's arm. "No, please. Finish your drink." Not feeling the touch of another human being for so long, it caused a tingling shock wave throughout her body and she pulled away. The fresh mugs were delivered.

Nora sensed no harm. The woman simply wanted to talk. She was just a lonely soul longing to engage in simple discussion with another person. In a peculiar sort of way, she related with the woman's plight and sat back down.

The woman smiled and offered her hand, "I'm Tanya."

"Charlene." The women shook hands.

Nora never had enjoyed a conversation packed with such meaningless small talk before. There were no accusations, no "I'm better than you" attitude; only plain chit chat. Like what she had witnessed those two women in the coffee shop do — tangerine pants and grape top, minus the judgment. Topics spanned from childhood adventures, teenage escapades, pets, relationships and whatever else. Tanya's storytelling skills were remarkable and

Nora wiped tears of laughter from her eyes and kept clearing her throat. She couldn't recall experiencing such emotional abandonment; not since being a child.

Nora remembered how the Collins family experienced little drama compared to a lot of other families. How much simpler life had been back when she was growing up. But she quickly scolded herself for surrendering to the over-used and inaccurate cliché. Of course there were the expected inconveniences of life: the resident neighborhood bullies, bathroom floods that ruined favorite record albums, the loss of two cherished cats to coyotes, and fights with her baby brother who teased her unmercifully and always snooped in her bedroom with his best friend, Daniel.

When prodded, Nora shared a few of her own stories, but Tanya possessed the "talking gene."

After a couple hours, and one too many beers, Nora consulted her watch. Guilt hit like a sledgehammer. What kind of parent, well, surrogate parent, was she — out drinking at 3:30 in the afternoon while Toby lay at home by himself! "I really must go."

"Yeah, me too. Gotta get to my shrink's office," Tanya slurred.

"You're going to your shrink like this?"

"Oh the sessions are way better when I'm not sober." She used a compact to apply pink lipstick, way beyond her natural lips. "Makes him feel like he's not making any headway. Ha ha!"

"Is he?"

"Is he what?" said Tanya wiping smudged mascara from beneath her eyes.

Nora grinned. "Is he making any headway?"

"Only when I tell him shit I've never told anyone else." Nora was silent. "You ever do things you've kept secret?"

"Of course, everyone has," Nora said.

"My shrink tells me sharing something loosens the grip it has on you. I'm clinging to that unlikely possibility." Not allowing herself to be sucked into the mire of her past mistakes, she lifted her almost empty glass and Nora reciprocated. "Here's to coming clean."

Their glasses clinked, they finished their drinks and stood, both swaying a bit. Nora turned back to her improbable new friend whom she would never see again. "It was good to meet you, Tanya."

"You too, Charlene...or whatever your real name is." Nora stared. "No worries, honey. We're all running from something. Hey, you might go brunette next time." She tugged at one side of Nora's synthetic hair to straighten the wig. "Blonde is definitely not your color, sweetie."

"But —"

Tanya waved her hand dismissing the protest. "We all wear disguises. The hard part is wearing one that actually looks real."

CHAPTER 49

A winter storm created foreboding skies and the unceasing rain soaked Nora's sweatshirt and jeans despite her attempt to stay dry under an established oak tree and a piece of discarded cardboard. Early mid-December morning temperatures held in the low forties. She wore sunglasses in the gloomy weather and had the black hood tightened around her face.

Unsure if the cause of her sneezing came from an impending cold or was cedar fever, she decided it most likely the latter since she suffered from it for the past three years along with many other Austenites. It was a unique and very common allergy stemming from inhaling the pollen from the prevalent mountain cedar trees during certain months. Nora sneezed again and rubbed her itchy eyes realizing that would be a constant irritant until February or March.

Perhaps the time had come to leave Texas altogether. But unless she scored the desperately needed supplies, she didn't see that happening anytime soon. At least a hundred times Nora scolded herself for not bringing more batteries from the start. She should have asked more questions of Amisha about how long they lasted.

Her hopes remained high that things might change that day as she stood thirty yards from a red-lettered sign.

PRIVATE PROPERTY, NO TRESPASSING

The parking area was under-sized for the massive warehouse structure with windowless walls. The signage out front indicated it was the Postponement Center's Central Facility where so many postponed lives lie waiting to be reunited with their families.

Nora delayed as long as possible before coming to Central accepting the uncertain chance of exposure. She managed to stay under the radar so far and figured she had no other options. A Sunday meant very few employees. Usually only one or two came in to catch up on paperwork or prep for upcoming busy weeks. Emergency postponements always went to the location in which Nora had worked.

She waited for an hour to find out who might arrive to work that day. A Volvo turned into the driveway. It belonged to the last person she wanted to encounter.

After the driver gathered her purse and some files, Nora dropped the soggy box lid to the ground and jogged over to the back of the car to wait. The door opened, an umbrella raised, and out stepped a woman.

"Kathy."

The woman jumped in surprise and whirled around. "This is private property," she said in a gruff tone. "You cannot —" She stopped when the sunglasses came off. "Nora? Where have you been and where is that baby?"

"I'm asking for your help."

"No way, I'm not getting mixed up in anything that —"

"I just want to talk." She moved forward causing Kathy to back away. She lifted her arms showing there was no threat. "Can we please sit in your car? I'm wet to the bone."

"Are you carrying a weapon?" her old coworker asked noticing the front pocket in Nora's drenched sweatshirt.

"Of course not."

Kathy considered then got back into her car and unlocked the passenger side permitting Nora to climb into the toasty interior. "Do you even realize what you've done?"

"I know. I need a few supplies."

"He's still in his crypod?"

Nora nodded. "Three or four batteries would work." She brushed rainwater from her face as the windows began to fog.

It took a good ten seconds for the shock of the request to register with Kathy. Her response was curt. "You're pretty ballsy, expecting me to participate in your kidnapping scheme."

"I didn't kidnap him."

Kathy gave an audible scoff. "What would you call it, then?"

"I'm just taking care of him for a while."

"This is a business, not a baby-sitting service." Nora did not respond. "You endangered a neonate — a life that doesn't belong to you."

"Tob..." she corrected herself, "The baby is not in danger. However, I really need these things. Don't do it for me, do it for the child."

Kathy shook her head, not believing who was sitting in her car. She could lock the doors and drive straight to the authorities. "Just because you're stupid, doesn't mean I am. I actually don't want to be sent to prison."

Nora massaged her temples underneath her dampened hood, a few hair strands from a dark brown wig fell loose and emerged. "No one has to know, you can —"

"Get out of my car," Kathy said, abruptly.

"Please."

"I said get out."

With a final cold stare, Nora opened the car door and re-emerged into the heavy rain. Leaning back in she said, "You don't understand."

Kathy frantically dug in her bag for her cell phone. Once found, she hit one button and put it up to her ear while staring at Nora. "I have information about the missing Martinez baby."

Nora sprinted from the lot wishing she had on her running shoes. The next random bus that came by, she boarded and traveled for a while before exiting and finding the correct route back home.

The to-and-fro swaying and stop-and-go motion during the long ride, lulled Nora into reflective contemplation. She felt tired and burdened. Kathy didn't understand. *Perhaps I should sneak into TPC and steal what I need.* That idea evaporated rather quick as she realized the absurdity of breaking in without getting caught and arrested. Nora was not a true criminal regardless of all the accusations claimed by the media.

The brakes squealed and she exited. At least the downpour had ceased, replaced with light sprinkles. A wide river of water flowed down the street and in deep drains. As she walked, Nora decided she just needed to pay close attention to the batteries to try and prolong their life.

She approached the motel and saw ten people assembled on the front sidewalk. When rounding the corner to take the dirt path, she stopped short. A half dozen police cars were spread across the lot. Officers held rifles and handguns pointed towards her room. Another crowd stood ready to capture any action on their phone cameras.

Nora retreated pressing her back against the stuccoed wall of a pawn shop. Should she run? Should she stay? She chewed her lower lip and from somewhere, she mustered up enough courage to take a peek.

CHAPTER 50

Edging along the walkway of the bottom level rooms were six uniformed and armed men, three on each side. They communicated with stiff hand signals as the two groups grew closer to room 111, Nora's room.

Her heart pounded out of her chest and she cupped her face in her hands. What would she do if they took Toby? She could disappear by moving to some obscure little town or obtain a fake passport and cross the border into Mexico, but that would mean allowing the authorities, the press, everyone to believe she intended to take and keep Toby. No one knew of her true intentions — except maybe, Ruben. The police froze right outside her door and Nora did not flinch.

In a flash, one hefty officer burst through the flimsy room door and several officers flooded inside. Wait. They entered room 112, the room next door.

Nora's eyes widened and she did not breathe. It would not take long to discover they had the wrong room. Then they would search them all and find the unit hidden under the blanket and duffle bag only twenty feet away. How had they found her? It must have been Kathy, but how so soon?

After about a minute, the officers began emerging from the room, two of them escorted out a shirtless man in handcuffs. He was a skinny guy with long straggly hair. Nora witnessed him going in and out of his room several times over the previous few days.

Nora's anxiety diminished as she watched the man being put into the back of a squad car and driven away. Two policemen lingered for another fifteen minutes while the clerk on duty was pumped for facts. After they left and most of the lookie-loos wandered away, Nora returned to her room. She secured the door, tore over to Toby and stared down at him, her fingers running along the top of the crypod that functioned in perfect condition.

The stress of the afternoon overcame her and she began sobbing. "I'm sorry, Toby. I'm so sorry." She never wanted anything to happen to him and what was she doing taking chances with this little boy's life. Nora must be more vigilant and vowed that she wouldn't leave him for any long periods of time anymore; unless it was an absolute necessity. She was getting too sloppy.

CHAPTER 51

Michael dragged himself to his car after 1:00 a.m. to begin his trek home. Preparing for a client's audit always required an exorbitant amount of time and he dreaded the impending meeting with the Internal Revenue Service agent in seven short hours.

A radio program recapped the latest scores for the baseball playoffs and basketball kickoff games. The only advantage of working late was the lack of traffic. A normal commute home took over sixty-five minutes, but at that awful hour, the ride was cut in half.

He waited at one of the many downtown signals. An older blue pickup raced through the intersection, slipping through the yellow light. Michael noticed it resembled his own even though the woman driving had long dark brown hair. He considered a moment and on the green, instead of going straight, he turned right. Curiosity teasing him.

Michael sped to catch up, but they both got stuck stopping again, the truck one signal ahead. The stoplights changed simultaneously and he accelerated until right behind the Chevy.

"Well, I'll be damned," he said, recognizing the plates. He crossed lanes so when they hit the next red light, their vehicles sat next to each other. Never mind the brunette color, he knew his sister's profile.

Nora glanced over and saw Michael looking at her. She froze, not reacting nor making any facial expressions. They held eye-contact until she looked forward again unable to process the situation. She peered to her passenger seat, then back to her brother. He lowered his vehicle window, motioning for her to do the same; however, she remained still.

Not fully understanding her actions or mindset, Michael did not force the issue. He could always count on his sister to handle things through avoidance, jetting away as fast as she possible in the opposite direction; like if she simply turned a blind eye, things would somehow improve on their own. But, he did love her, no matter how unreasonable she might be at times and he pushed down his irritation like usual.

Nora stared at him as if attempting to communicate through no words at all. In that moment, through her exhausted tired eyes, Michael recognized unselfish passion, her belief that her behaviors were right. Although he was unsure that those choices were the best way of handling whatever it was she was trying to accomplish, at least she did something, made a stand, carried through with a difficult decision.

Michael experienced an odd settled feeling and he smiled at her. His reward came as the smallest tinge of a smile was reciprocated. Then Nora turned right and drove away. He did not follow — contented that she understood how much he loved her.

Tears fell from Nora's eyes as she missed Michael's irritating and obnoxious ways. She wanted nothing more than to stop, grab a drink and explain herself. Perhaps even enjoy a hug and show him Toby's sweet face. But doing so would have endangered Michael. He must not be a party to anything.

Ten minutes later, she checked in another motel and parked at the back of the building near her assigned room. A bottom level room was always requested, yet sometimes she had to accept a second floor. Tonight that happened. Two cars down, three college aged kids milled around. One girl sat on the hood of the car while both boys stood. They shared a joint and drank from bottles of beer.

Nora did not exit out of her car and wondered what to do. She needed to transfer Toby to the room, yet not in front of these people. At first she stalled pretending to be searching for something in her purse. Several minutes passed and the group continued joking and now smoked cigarettes while passing around a whiskey bottle.

Struggling to remain unsuspicious, Nora took everything, except Toby, and slipped in her room. From inside she could keep an eye out, waiting for them to leave. An hour ticked by and a battery change became crucial so she re-emerged and returned to her truck.

Nora unhooked the canvas strapped rigging system she had devised to hold the crypod securely to the seat to prevent any mishaps from occurring from an unexpected slam of the brakes. Using the green cover, she wrapped it tight around the unit. Her foot slammed the door closed and she lugged the bundle towards the stairs.

"Watcha got there? You need some help?" called out one of the guys. Avoiding the question, she began her ascent.

"Hey lady, he's just being polite," said the girl, "You don't have to be so rude."

Almost to the top step, the other guy yelled, "Got something valuable there? You sneaking something around?"

"Yeah, you must be. Why don't you tell us what's under the blanket," said the first.

The woman added, "Come on, we wanna —"

Nora placed the crypod on the dresser before closing and bolting the door. She quickly replaced the battery putting the depleted one on to recharge. She was too riled to unpack further and left the lights off.

Through the window, she watched the little troublemakers who kept talking and glancing at her room. They partied on while she withdrew a well-worn piece of paper from a zippered backpack pocket. It was delicate to the touch, soft from all the folding and unfolding. She examined it by the dull rays of exterior light shining through the split in the curtains. Nora had gone into a local library branch early on and researched a list of at least forty motels around Austin, San Antonio and many of the surrounding smaller towns that fit the requirements. Over three-quarters of the location names had lines drawn through them. Either she had stayed in them already or they had refused to buy her excuse of losing her driver's license and turned down her offer of cash. With more time to plan she might have secured fraudulent identification.

Ninety long minutes elapsed. The three dawdlers finally left, after which Nora loaded all her belongings back in the Chevy and left as well.

CHAPTER 52

A rerun of *A Charlie Brown's Christmas* flickered. Nora had watched when a child, but had not seen the program in decades. Obviously it still held appeal because the show played every December since the mid-sixties.

"Everything I do turns into a disaster," Snoopy claimed. Nora chuckled.

She laid atop the bed in a well-worn T-shirt and sweat pants forced at the seams from her expanding thighs. Her hand went in and out of a bag of Doritos Nacho Cheese chips. A can of Pepsi sat within arm's reach on the bedside table.

Nora scratched her scalp where four inches of natural gray hair ended abruptly at her original dyed color of mousy brown. Her grooming standards had relaxed over the previous few months. She justified to herself that it would make her harder to recognize, but if honest, she recognized the signs, all too well, as depression. The right leg tucked under her left started to numb and she shifted positions trying to find some semblance of fluff in the cheap over-used pillows.

Tired of yet another commercial, Nora found the remote and changed channels. She stopped upon seeing her face filling the screen. Still the same work photograph. She hated that picture! No smile, unemotional eyes. One that made everyone think of her as a horrible, dreadful, baby-stealing woman. It had been a while since anything aired about the situation thanks to other daily tragedies capturing the headlines.

The news reporter stood alone with The Postponement Center as the backdrop. "This should be the Martinezes' first holiday with their child. Nora Collins has prevented that."

Nora's eyes moved to Toby's crypod. For the past week she fought off the urge to let Ruben know his son was safe. Perhaps she should drop off another note; however, last time did not turn out well. She acknowledged the anguish the parents were experiencing because of her actions, but they must understand everything was for their son's own benefit.

The reporter continued. "The police are following up on a lead from last week in the hunt for this kidnapper. It now appears that Collins may have remained hiding somewhere in Austin or the surrounding cities." The camera panned as the microphone went up in front of Kathy.

Nora kicked herself. She knew not to trust that woman. Why had she taken the risk? Feeling antsy and nervous, she switched off the television, got up and began pacing.

Earlier the maintenance guy smiled and waved as she returned with some groceries. She had stayed too long. Perhaps the move might wait until tomorrow, yet she could not chance the daylight. Every time she moved her desire grew stronger to splurge for a night at a Holiday Inn Express or even a Hampton Inn — both luxurious compared to how she was living. But that would be impossible. Outside access was essential and cash must talk louder than policy.

Checking on the crypod status, the recharging battery reflected half-full and the current one at thirty-two percent; it was enough to withstand another move. She selected a motel not too far away which was good since she felt beyond exhausted for no reason at all.

Nora began the perfunctory packing to which she had become so accustomed. She slipped into the dark sweatshirt and pushed her uncombed hair up into the hood. The clothes were shoved into her bag and the three remaining canisters, recharger and second battery slid into her back pack. Waiting until after midnight, she, Toby, and her meager possessions were secured in Michael's blue truck and headed towards the highway.

The unit power level drained at a gradual rate, although after so many moves, Nora understood there was enough time to stop for some dinner.

With a multitude of fast food restaurants willing to feed her inexpensive, artery-hardening nutrition, she didn't struggle with finding one. After driving through, she parked near the back of the lot. Her eyes glazed over while shoveling in skinny hot french-fries and biting into a grease-dripping bacon cheeseburger. She chewed mechanically washing everything down with gulps of Coke.

Nora opened her wallet and rummaged through the bills inside. There appeared to still be plenty and more was hidden in bag pockets. She had been a model saver, never spending any money without need or valid reason. Her non-existent social life ensured the freedom to act upon an unanticipated decision to do something significant. Granted most people her age struggled to put away for their future, Nora avoided thinking about retirement. How could she?

She brushed salt from her lap and stared out the window at a woman and two middle-school aged boys. They all carried bags of food and the mother unlocked her car with a beep.

For the hundredth time Nora thought about how to return Toby to his parents. It must be on her terms, not theirs.

Calls to Erin had stopped in fear she might turn her in. Instead periodic visits to utilize library computers helped keep her somewhat abreast of how the research was progressing. She became quite adept at reading medical journals and reports. In her estimate, holding on for another six to eight months, might be enough for the needed procedures to be available, at least in an experimental method. Toby was the pawn in the whole mess. But Nora refused to do anything pre-maturely because of her own selfishness.

She checked the charge again. A fifth left, she better get moving.

Within twenty minutes, she entered another motel and mindlessly progressed through the routine. She lugged the blanket-covered crypod in first placing it on the desk. On the bed were the duffle, backpack, purse and a paper sack. Next the do-not-disturb tag was displayed, and the door was closed and bolted. Opening the dresser, she dumped clothes into a heap, then spread the wrinkled and disorganized items out to enable the drawer to close.

The room stunk like old cigars. Nora took to burning a scented candle to mask the odors often wafting throughout the rooms. She ignited a match and lit a green one. The label touted pine trees, but the fragrance was more reminiscent of fermenting cut grass. It didn't matter. Anything was better than what might have been happening there an hour before she arrived.

Out from the grocery bag came a four-pack of individual serving red wine. She flopped on the padded chair next to Toby and unscrewed the first. Long gone was her stigma about drinking alcohol straight from a plastic bottle.

Nora touched the side of the misty crypod while melting into a flood of thought. The ever-present gurgling was hardly audible any longer — the sound that for so long brought her comfort while at TPC. She believed that Toby sensed her presence even though her words to him had lessened. Perhaps a small tree and a few ornaments would cheer them both up.

Her own mother obsessed over decorations every year, insisting that Nora's father string up colored lights to every house eve and front-yard bush. Fake frost sprayed around the edges of every window and the fresh green wreath was arranged and affixed to their front door. Nora smiled remembering the mistletoe hung in the kitchen doorway created some awkward moments. Toby would like a tree, just a little one.

Nora fell into a dreamy sleep filled with strange, nonsensical dreams. As she slumbered, the candle snuffed itself out. The blue light popped off.

CHAPTER 53

Nora moved in the chair, her back stiff. She heard a muffled sound. Must be another commercial. Through one unfocused eye she forced open, she saw the dark television screen. Rubbing both eyes, three empty wine bottles came clear. Still groggy she pushed herself up and glanced to the room door. What could that noise be?

Her head turned to the crypod. There was no blue light so she blinked a few times and looked again. That couldn't be! Still no blue light. Her eyes darted to the battery. It showed black. No green. No charge!

She bolted to stand over the unit. "No!" she said, her eyes growing large at the realization of what the sound was or more aptly, who it was coming from. Inside, Toby's face contorted as he bawled his eyes out.

Nora punched some buttons on the keypad, the lid unlatched with a click and when she yanked it open, a cool puff of air hit her face. The technology had performed flawlessly by providing the consummate mixture of oxygen, nitrogen, water vapor and other essential gases to keep its precious cargo safe. The baby's body lay covered in a thick bluish-green chemical and his fragile hands scrunched into fists.

With a towel, she gathered him up wrapping him tight all while murmuring soothing words. "Shh, shh, it's okay, honey. Yes, alright now, Toby."

The rocking and talking began to quiet him down, her eyes filled. All those years at TPC, he recognized her voice only, not Sylvia's, not Ruben's, nor anyone else's. She knew him and he knew her. Nora brushed the gooey matter from his cheek using her finger. After so many years, this boy was awake. Toby lie in her arms. She brought the swaddled infant up to her face and kissed his warm forehead then pressed her own cheeks into the towel blotting away her tears.

Nora experienced a wave of unexplainable joy — the bliss of a mother when holding her newborn baby for the very first time. She managed to remain under everybody's noses for months and never got caught. No one could care for him as much and the sliver of an idea she had been suppressing from the start became tangible. *No one would know if I kept him.*

She carried Toby in the bathroom and turned on the water spigots allowing steam to heat the room. Nora cradled the calm child in one arm and seemed to enjoy the tepid sponge-bath that washed away the substance from his face, inside the tiny creases of his ears, off the bronze color of his chest and arms, and from between his delicate fingers.

"You're beautiful," whispered Nora. She continued speaking to him in a hushed motherly way about being perfect, a miracle, little Toby.

He watched with relaxed deep brown eyes as she smiled, cooed and made over-emphasized expressions.

Desiring to clean him thoroughly, she placed a bath towel on the counter. Once on his back, he began to wail, his arms flailing. His legs were slack, unmoving. Both exhibited a bright red tinge to them under the colored goop.

Nora snapped from her fantasy world back to a harsh reality. "No." She picked Toby up, holding him close to her chest attempting to comfort him. She swiped away a strip of condensation from the mirror to view the blurry reflection of his back. A bulge protruded where the spine had not fused. A raw bundle of nerves were exposed. He screamed.

The shower and sink water remained running as Nora wrapped Toby in her soft black ASU sweatshirt hanging on a hook, then bundled more fresh towels around him. Carrying him into the main room, she grabbed her keys, her purse, the green blanket and rushed out of the motel room. The door slammed hard leaving behind the now dark, silent and defunct crypod. The water vapors continued to pour out from the bathroom.

Nora put the blanket on the passenger side floorboard. She snuggled Toby amidst the folds propping him on his side. His long lashes moved up and down, his lids becoming heavy.

Her hands shook but there was no doubt about what had become necessary. As she pulled from the parking lot, she withdrew an unused cell which she had purchased only for urgent situations. This qualified and she dialed letting it ring multiple times. Nora's eyes alternated between the road and Toby who had fallen fast asleep with the motion of the vehicle.

The phone was answered. "It's me," said Nora.

CHAPTER 54

It was the middle of the night. The emergency room held only a handful of other patients awaiting their turn. A skinny Colorado blue spruce stood in the corner with twinkling red and white lights and sporadic purple and green ornaments. The colors from the tree reflected off the glass doors as they slid open.

Nora entered with a gush of cold night air. She clung to Toby and scanned the room until she spotted a familiar face rushing towards her. Erin wore jeans and a bulky jacket. Unbrushed hair and no makeup made her plain as a vanilla bean — rare, but obvious that she had been summoned in a hurry.

As the women approached each other, Nora began first. "He needs —"

"Got it," Erin said, motioning to an ER nurse who hurried over.

"Come this way," the staff member directed starting to lead them down the corridor.

"That is my baby!" came a sharp yell from behind them. Nora glared at Erin. Her betrayal hitting hard. Sylvia ran up with Ruben following. A fire was burning in her eyes as she screamed, "He's mine!"

Nora swallowed, then relinquished Toby to his mother.

"How could you —" Sylvia started, but once her eyes fell upon her son for the first time, she became speechless. Overjoyed and overwhelmed all in a single moment, her child consumed her. The nurse tugged on Sylvia's arm escorting her down the hallway. Nora's gaze never left the infant — the little boy she had tried to help and whom she would never set eyes on again.

Ruben touched her shoulder. His eyes were glassy and she didn't know if he wanted to scream at her or hug her. After some moments of uncertainty, a small, grateful smile broached his lips.

"Ruben," came a voice and he turned around. "My name is Erin." He reached out and they shook hands and when he looked back to Nora, she was gone.

Erin motioned for him to catch up with his wife and he scurried off while she went back to the entrance. She saw Nora shift into gear and drive away in Michael's truck.

CHAPTER 55

Nora sat at the end of the counter at a local bar not far from the hospital. A few patrons milled around on the late Tuesday night, or rather Wednesday morning, a half hour before the 2:00 a.m. closing time.

One inebriated couple flirted as they battled over a game of billiards, and a guy wearing a beanie rested his head on a table already dreaming away. However, Nora noticed nothing as she studied the melting ice cubes in her depleted glass.

"Here you go," said the bartender serving another straight up Jack Daniels. "You been in here, before? I'm pretty good at remembering faces and you look like I've served you before."

After no answer, he tried to remove the empty tumbler but she slapped her hand down hard on the rim, her eyes still glued to it. He stepped back raising both eyebrows and went to do his last call. Erin witnessed this from behind and slipped on the stool next to her former liaison without saying a word.

Nora did not raise her head. "You found me," she said, her tone flat and deflated.

"How many blue classic pickups do you see these days?" Erin remarked as Nora sucked long sips of the amber refreshment. "I never thought you'd handle things this way, Nora."

"Why did you call Sylvia?"

"Because it was their child and they needed to be there." The bartender returned and Erin pointed to Nora's glass. "One of those." He nodded and walked away.

Erin eyed the graying hair and made an attempt at humor to cut the unbearable tension. "Someone could use a visit to the salon." No response came and the seat squeaked when Erin squirmed. "Honestly, what do you think I can do for these people? You put me in a pretty shitty position, here." Nora remained silent. "Do you even feel the slightest bit guilty about what you did?"

The previous ninety minutes had prompted some perspective for Nora. Her intention never was to harm but only help the most defenseless person involved — Toby. Yet, things had not turned out at all like she imagined. Once the complete cure had been developed, she planned to deliver the functioning crypod back to TPC. She shrugged. "Everything I've done is now wasted. The parents will sue. Thompson will file charges. And the worst thing about all this...." Swallowing another gulp, she allowed the throat burn without a flinch. "...The medical treatment isn't even ready now that Toby's awake."

"Awake?" Erin repeated, puzzled. "He wasn't sleeping." The women sat in silence both mindlessly looking at the television. An over-used, traditional early morning video played. A program entitled, *The Top 20 Epic Fails*. Number eleven showed some guy attempting a flip into a pool, but landing face first back on the diving board. Nora wondered how people found such programing entertaining. Erin's drink arrived and she took a taste then squeezed her eyes shut. "Wow."

"Why are you here?"

Erin tilted her head. "We're friends."

"You pity me."

"What?"

"I have no friends."

"That's not true," said Erin. "Why won't you let me in? You've got to trust people."

Nora stared nowhere for a long time waiting for the alcohol to dull the pain. "I had been accepted into med school."

"I didn't know that. What happened?"

"Nora Collins?" came a man's voice from behind them.

Both women turned to two uniformed officers, hands resting on their holstered guns. Nora furrowed her brow. "You called the police, too?"

Erin shook her head, "No." She caught the bartender's eye before he quickly averted his attention. He had indeed recognized the kidnapper.

Nora nodded at the men and stood placing her hands behind her back. She closed her eyes.

"You are under arrest for the kidnapping of Ruben and Sylvia Martinez' baby," said one as the other locked the handcuffs.

One officer began reciting Miranda rights as they escorted Nora away. "You have the right to remain silent. Anything you say can and will be used against you in a court of law. You have the right to an attorney. If you cannot afford an attorney, one will be provided for you —"

Things fell into a slow-motion, dreamy blur.

CHAPTER 56

For the next twelve hours, Nora's life proceeded with no particular thoughts. Her mind was blank, her emotions were numb; she was just going through the motions. She had been handcuffed, finger printed, mug shot, strip-searched, and jostled into a cold cell. Later she was dragged out and stood in front of a late night judge where, due to her being a high flight risk, her bail was set at one million dollars. When led from the courtroom, Nora spotted Michael. After passing through a crowd of shouting reporters thrusting microphones and cameras towards her, she was herded into a windowless van and the door was slammed.

On the bumpy trip to the jail house, images of Toby filled her head. What might happen to him? Would he ever understand her sacrifices? She acknowledged she would never see him again. This was what she deserved and she deserved everything she would get. So many people had looked foolish because of her actions, yet, she felt certain in her heart that she would do it all over.

Three days later, dressed in elastic waist-banded white pants and a loose top, Nora waited in a small room. It was such a stark contrast from the conference room in which she had spent thousands of hours at The Postponement Center. There were no fresh flowers or fragrant room freshener, no filtered water or crystal goblets, and the walls were void of child photographs. Here, only a marred wooden table and two uncomfortable gray plastic chairs were present.

Nora was left alone for over thirty minutes before the door opened. "No, I'll be fine, thank you," came the voice of a small-framed woman in her mid-thirties.

"We'll be right here," said a guard standing outside the sealed room.

The woman closed the door. Shoulder-length blond hair was clipped into a short ponytail. She plunked an overstuffed leather case on the table, settled in across from the prisoner, and offered her hand. "Hello, Nora" she said with a heavy Texan drawl. "I'm Treaty Nayblush." Her handshake was solid. "Michael asked me to come."

The smallest hint of a smile touched Nora's lips.

CHAPTER 57

Treaty opened the briefcase removing a manila folder already growing thick with papers. Then she removed her blazer and hung it on the back of her chair.

Nora noticed the white label in the neckline of the woman's grey and white patterned jacket: ARMANI COLLEZIONI, Made in Italy. Confident that was not a designer sold at the local Kohl's where Nora used to do her clothes shopping before Goodwill, she hoped it was an indication of Ms. Nayblush's experience level. "How do you know, Michael?"

Treaty smiled the smile of an orthodontist's child. "We attended a few of the same financial conferences." Nora mused why her brother had not tried to woo this woman instead of Bree, but that answer became apparent with the sheen from the rock on her left fourth finger. "As soon as you called him, he got in touch with me to see if I would represent you." Treaty slid over her business card. The woman was indeed a defense attorney with a prestigious firm in Austin. Nora had seen their company name atop a fancy stone building downtown.

Unsure if it would help or hinder, Nora asked, "Do you have children, Treaty?"

"In fact, I do. A five-year-old boy and a three-year-old girl. And yes, they are a handful."

Michael would not have sent her someone that was not trustworthy. "I don't know much about how the legal process works. I'm more of a nature show lover," said Nora.

Opening the file, Treaty said, "That's why I'm here," and she patted Nora's hand. Nora pulled her hand back placing it into her lap. "Sorry, I'm kind of a touchy type."

Nora cast her eyes down. "Well, I'm guilty so I guess it shouldn't be too complicated."

The attorney held up her hand, "Hold on, now. Let's start with you telling me what happened."

"You don't know? I'm sure it has been all over the news."

"I want to hear it from you, not from the spin the media puts on it. Tell me from your perspective and don't leave anything out."

Out came the entire story about Toby and her attempt to help him. As she did, it sounded like some suspense novel and she couldn't believe she had been the lead character — the protagonist. Or perhaps as some saw her — the antagonist.

Treaty remained engaged and listened with an attentive ear periodically jotting down notes. After Nora finished, the attorney lowered her Montblanc pen. "I appreciate you being so thorough."

Nora awaited Treaty's response.

"The police have presented the case to the prosecution and they've filed the official complaint. Criminal kidnapping charges are severe and very unforgiving. But you'd be astonished how many defendants are exonerated because of technicalities. Officer's not following proper proced —"

"But, I am guilty," Nora said, resigned to the fact she would likely spend many years in prison. "Why prolong this anymore?"

Her attorney leaned forward in her chair, "Why don't you let me make the decision of how best to proceed here?"

"I don't want to be put on display. I want to accept my punishment and move on."

Treaty cocked her head, rose to her feet and wandered from one side of the small room to the other and back. Her hand stroked her chin and eyes raised to the ceiling. *A typical lawyer stance*, thought Nora. "There are a few things in our favor."

"How could that be?"

Treaty processed her contemplation out loud, more for Nora's benefit. "Even though you intentionally abducted the neonate, you did not demand a ransom, hold him hostage, inflict any bodily injury on him and you did not use any kind of weapon."

"I would never have hurt him." Nora shook her head. "I kept him safe."

"But, you did interfere with the performance of police recovery efforts." Nora agreed with that truth. Five months of evading the authorities could not be favorable.

Treaty continued. "Frankly, there is no precedents for what happened. Legally, a neonate is not recognized as a person nor an individual and is not considered a real life but rather is the sole property of the parents."

Nora was appalled. "Of course he is a *real* life. He's a child."

Treaty ceased pacing. "Yes, I realize that. It's just that the law defines *alive* as being born. And, you returned the neonate —-"

"Could you please not refer to him as a neonate?" insisted Nora.

Treaty gave a wary look, then acquiesced. "You returned the baby immediately upon his reanimation and I think there might be some wiggle room." She smiled as she sat back down across from her client. "Enough wiggle room for a plea bargain, that is if you insist on pleading guilty," Nora delivered a vehement confirming nod. "Prosecutors like guilty pleas because it is a guaranteed conviction without all the hassle of court. But they must give up something."

"What's that?"

"We'll try to get them to agree to drop some of the charges and for a lighter sentence. Maybe they'll go for just extended parole."

Nora sighed. Could that even be possible? She crossed her arms and stared at Treaty.

CHAPTER 58

Two weeks later Nora was escorted into a courtroom. Sylvia and Ruben Martinez sat near the front with Erin seated next to them. Sylvia held a slumbering Toby although his face was not visible. She resisted the urge to smile at the bundle of blue.
Treaty Nayblush informed her that The Postponement Center lawyers had convinced the Martinezes that Nora had acted on her own behalf and not as a representative of their corporation. In exchange for their agreement not to sue the company, the parents accepted a hefty private settlement. The couple decided not to file a personal complaint against Nora either which shocked her.

Also amongst the crowd of strangers was Dr. Leonard Thompson. He had not filed charges either. "Probably determined it would create more negative attention for his organization," explained Treaty.

Michael came into Nora's line of sight. He gave his sister a wink and wave of his hand.

As Nora sat down next to her lawyer who was dressed in an expensive Michael Kors business suit, she glanced over to the prosecuting attorney — his head down examining papers in front of him.

Then her attention fell upon Judge McArthur, a plump man graying at the temples. His dark eyes pierced Nora and she felt her heart speed up. Treaty had described him as one of the toughest judges for acquiescing to lawyer negotiated plea bargains.

"Ms. Collins," he began. "Prosecution has agreed to the presented plea bargain for reduced charges and also on a lesser sentence in lieu of longer probation. I understand you intend to plead guilty to the counts being brought against you. Is this accurate?"

"Yes sir," said Nora. Judge McArthur went on to ask a series of rote questions about foregoing any trial rights. She answered just how her attorney had coached her to respond.

"All right, Ms. Collins. I accept to forego a trial and to the reducing of charges due to your lack of criminal history, your prompt return at reanimation of the unharmed infant beyond his original medical birth issues, the fact that the parents nor your past employer have chosen to press charges, as well as your admitted remorse for your actions. The court is accepting the reduction from a third degree felony for kidnapping to a Class A misdemeanor. Prior to handing down your formal sentence, do you wish to say anything?"

"Yes, thank you," Nora said, standing and clenching her trembling hands together. "I realize what I did was not right and I created a lot of problems." She turned looking directly at the Martinez family. "I sincerely apologize for the worry I caused you." Tears over-flowed from Nora's eyes as Sylvia rocked Toby back and forth in her arms. "What I did was only and always for the safety and well-being of your son." Treaty placed her hand on her client's elbow prompting her to sit down.

Sylvia did not blink and Ruben put his arm around his wife. Michael tightened his tie in an unconscious effort to trap his emotions inside.

"Ms. Collins, I understand your misguided conduct as intended to help the infant, albeit in a very unconventional way," said Judge McArthur. "However, I do not see this as a crime to go unpunished and am rejecting the sentence agreed to by counsel. Taking a neonate from the protection of your employer's facility and putting him at potentially great risk remains a serious offense in my eyes. Ruben and Sylvia Martinez suffered unimaginable anguish for five months not knowing the whereabouts of their child or even if he was dead or alive. Therefore, I hereby sentence you to serve one year in a Texas State Prison with no credit for early release and a fine of ten thousand dollars."

Nora remained stoic as she absorbed the harsh reality. Treaty leaned over and whispered, "It could have been much worse."

The thought of spending twelve months incarcerated produced an uneasiness in Nora's stomach. She would become a prisoner inside a cold cell, just like so many of the babies at The Postponement Center.

CHAPTER 59

The time inside began and continued. On some days, Nora maintained a sense of justification because her actions had honored her beliefs; however, remorse filled many hours as well. She often tried to imagine what her parents would say about their daughter being incarcerated. Her dreams were occupied with scoldings from her mother and a father who refused to speak to her.

On Michael's first visit, she explained the complete story to him leaving nothing out. Certain he would grace her with a multitude of snide comments, his reaction surprised her. He beamed and said, "This was the first thing I saw you actually follow through on in a really long time. You took charge." His eyes grew watery and he swallowed. "I'm proud of what you did, Sis."

Nora drew in and exhaled a long breath. During the entire exhaustive ordeal, no one had acknowledged her, not anyone in the whole long drawn out process. All the heaviness she carried — the accusations, the ridicule, the judgment had now been muted without warning by her brother's single statement. She loved him in that moment more than she ever thought possible and against all efforts not to cry, she started and could not stop.

Realizing he had not seen his older sister shed tears since they were children, Michael shifted in his seat and said, "Hey, the dude that makes the wine still wants to meet you. He doesn't have any kids."

Caught in mid-sob, Nora snorted, causing unrestrained laughter between the siblings. Grateful for the immediate lightening of the moment, she welcomed home the solace of her irritating and teasing brother. She looked forward to Michael's Wednesday afternoon visits. He never missed.

Three times Erin wrote claiming she wanted to be there for Nora. Dealing with her old client seemed too difficult, too painful, so the letters remained unanswered. Nora thought about how right Dr. Thompson had been with his warning about making friends with former clients. The "poster-mother" of postponement services wanted for nothing, found success in everything, and did anything she desired. But Nora could not ignore the fact that Erin was the one to call the Martinezes and likely led to her being trapped within those four walls. Yet again, if the parents had not been summoned, she might have spent years running and hiding. *What kind of life was that?* She let the complicated friendship go.

There existed so much, way too much, time to think on things. Nora mused about her past clients during her tenure at The Postponement Center and speculated what they thought of her now that she sat behind steel bars. She wondered how Stephany was getting along in her family with all those brothers and sisters, and a mother who cared less about her child than the extra tax deduction she generated.

She thought of Carl. Had he adjusted to his daughter being awarded to another couple? Are those adoptive parents spoiling her? What a wonderful possibility.

Then Thomas, dear Thomas and his mother, Tracy. Nora hoped his abusive father never found either of them.

How long would the Fullers keep their little girl "on ice?" as Michael described it. She imagined, once reanimated, Andy would provide the best for his little Adrianna so she would experience a storybook life developing into a beautiful and intelligent woman.

Nora also got an unanticipated note from Molly, her neighbor's teenager. It started out quite amusing,

Hi Ms. Collins. How are you? I've never written to anyone in the big house before.

Nora smiled and read on.

I just wanted to tell you that me and my boyfriend decided to keep our baby. He's a boy and we're trying to figure out what to call him. I like Cole but my bf likes Brent. There was something weird about the whole postponing thing. I mean it's okay, I guess, but we figured it wasn't something we'd do. You were super brave saving that baby. I won't see you again 'cuz we're moving back to Michigan to live with my grandma in a couple weeks. Thanks for telling us to go see the old lady from that non-profit place 'cuz it made us kinda think about things. Alright, well good luck, Ms. Collins. From Molly.

The most unexpected letter came from an E. Larson. Nora sat on her twin-sized cot puzzled over the correspondent whose return address reflected Austin. It was probably more hate-mail. She had received her share of that.

The door slid open with a clatter as Nora's cell mate stepped inside. "How'd it go?" The Russian woman in her mid-forties shook her head and plunked on her bed burying her face in the hard pillow.

Turned down three times now for early release, Galina already served over eight years of a fifteen-year sentence. The rough and tumble, heavy-accented woman had been convicted of reckless manslaughter after two teenagers died when Galina's car slammed into them. The judge offered no slack stating because, if not for her, those children would still be alive. Of no consequence was that her violent brother happened to be pursuing her with a gun.

Nora knew better than to attempt to comfort her celly. She said nothing further knowing Galina would talk when ready and not before. Her attention returned to her mail and she jumped to her feet upon opening it, beginning to pace in the small room. Rage fluttered in her chest and her breathing increased once learning the sender's identity.

Galina glanced up through reddened and dampened eyes. "What's going on?"

"This Emma woman," said Nora waving the typewritten page, "was one of the protesters that walked in front of my work. What audacity."

"Audacity?" questioned Galina, unsure of the meaning.

"She was bold enough to contact me. Probably preaching that taking Toby was wrong."

"It was."

"So does this make her feel more justified?" Nora said flopping onto her bed.

Galina put her hands behind her head. "You going to write back?"

"No."

Her cell mate held out her hand for the paper. "Zhenshchina." Nora had learned a few words in Russian, and zhenshchina meant 'woman', an endearment Galina often used. "You should come to anger class, today. You're too mad."

Nora grimaced not understanding the source of her annoyance with Emma having not read any of the woman's sentiments yet. She handed the letter over. After slow silent reading in her non-native language, Galina said, "She's talking of her childhood."

"I'm sure in some privileged family that never had any real life things happen to them."

Galina sat up frowning. "I don't understand."

Nora got back to her feet. "Some people act from obligation doing what they think is right and pushing their views on everyone else. But who says their way is the right way? This girl, who is barely a woman, shoved picket signs in the faces of desperate mothers and hurled hurtful, demeaning statements. How could she comprehend anything about postponing, let alone anything about me?"

"This woman?" said Galina handing the paper back. "It sounds like she was trying to protect the babies."

Nora collapsed on her thin mattress once more leaning against the wall. She had been attempting that as well — to protect the babies — one in particular. And here now she sat in prison.

"Give her a chance to understand," said Galina. When no response came, she laid back down, crossed her arms and closed her eyes.

After some consideration, Nora conceded and responded, if for no other reason than to justify her own behaviors.

Thus began several months of correspondence between the women — deep conversations about cultural norms and societal expectations. They forged through challenging subjects about the law, God, other people's choices and repercussions from those decisions. Emma's tone was always thought-provoking but nonaccusatory when Nora shared her viewpoints and reasoning on legal and moral issues. The established pen-pal relationship based itself upon honesty, mutual respect and compassion. One thing they agreed on: the world was not a perfect and ideal place.

Nora realized on many levels how they appeared completely opposite, but in reality, they were very much alike. Although quite unorthodox, she had followed through on her personal convictions, just as Emma had while carrying a hand-made protest sign. Both with lessons to learn, together they discovered they didn't need to label each other as right or wrong, but instead developed an ability to listen, discuss and consider.

Nora became accustomed to her routine in the state jail and writing with Emma helped the time pass. With three months left to serve, a thick envelope arrived containing words that penetrated all the assumptions and opinions formed about the young woman.

CHAPTER 60

Galina practiced her English by reading Emma's letter aloud. Her pace was slow with Nora assisting with more challenging words.

Dear Nora,
Thanks for your last letter and for explaining more about the history of why postponement was legalized. At fifteen, I was not aware of all the controversy. My parents got all worked up about it.

Honesty is so important and I think through all our letters we have earned each other's respect. Something else happened around that time that I want to tell you.

The summer before becoming a sophomore in high school, about forty of us went to church camp for a month. The bus ride to New Mexico was unbelievably long, like fourteen hours. The only good thing was an amazing hot seventeen-year-old guy named Chris who sat behind me. Being new to our church, he already was popular and all my friends liked him. Most boys didn't pay much attention to me because I acted kinda awkward. At least that's what my mother said. Anyway, Chris treated me so nice. He was so cool and actually interested in hearing about me and my five brothers and sisters and all our craziness. By the time we got there, we seemed pretty comfortable with each other.

We ended up hanging out a lot. He made me feel so different and told me I was beautiful, even though I knew it was a lie. Our camp had strict rules against any physical contact between boys and girls, like holding hands and kissing and stuff. Sort of lame but the counselors constantly watched us.

One day they drove us to a place to go on a hike. That was the first time we held hands between the seats. In fact, I had never held a boy's hand before except for my brothers. Then he pulled me behind a tree and kissed me. The sensation felt like no other and we both could hardly breathe. Later he confessed that though he had lots of friends, he had stayed pure — something many of us in the youth group vowed to do until marriage.

While packing on the last night, my roommates teased me that Chris and I would be a couple when we got home. I believed them and I couldn't stop smiling.

After everyone went to bed, I snuck out and Chris met me at our favorite spot by the lake. It was wonderful out there at midnight with the moon and stars shining so bright. He held my hand and we kissed. He was so gentle and warm.

One thing led to another and before I realized it, we were mostly undressed and doing things we weren't supposed to. Suddenly, we heard some of the staff people coming towards us and we rolled under the bushes pulling our clothes with us.

I never was so scared in my whole life.

They walked by and we were never caught. We got dressed and ran back to our cabins, but I couldn't sleep at all. I was shocked to get to that point with a boy; how could I do that? Remember, I was only fifteen. We easily might have had sex if those adults hadn't come by.

Chris must have been freaked out as well because when he boarded the bus, he walked by me and sat with his friends in the back. Once home, he kept his distance and we never found ourselves alone again. Which turned out fine for both of us. I was relieved when he changed churches with his family.

My parents would be devastated if they found out what happened. I focused a lot of my time trying to make up for it and make them proud of me which is what got me on that picket line at The Postponement Center in the first place. It became easy to point fingers at other people because nobody knew my own little secret.

I imagine this sounds like a stupid story compared to circumstances with people at your old work, but to me it still is huge. What I didn't want to ever admit, but couldn't ignore anymore is that you are right, sometimes things do happen. Even though I tried to believe my situation was different, it really wasn't.

I'm totally sitting here shaking now, because I've never said anything about this before. Not to my mom or any of my sisters, not even my best friend, and we tell each other everything! Now, I'm asking for you to share about something you never told to anyone before. My college small group leader wants us to find somebody to exchange a "confession of sin" with. I trust you and wanted you to be that person. Hopefully, you'll do the same.

Your friend.
Emma.

Galina refolded the papers and looked up. "What do you say?"

Nora used care not to outwardly process any internal comparisons. "Looks like she learned something about life."

"You going to send a sin back?"

"She's just a child."

"No. She's what, twenty-two? You need to share something with her."

"Why doesn't she talk to her mother or her friend?" said Nora getting to her feet, feeling annoyed.

"She needs it from you."

"I don't see how informing someone about a past mistake is such a big deal. Why bring up old wounds?"

"Because it helps. You have never been in therapy?"

"No."

Then Nora remembered drinking beer in the crusty bar with Tanya who told her, "Sharing something loosens the grip it has on you."

"Oh zhenshchina," said Galina, exasperated. "I'll tell you some of mine, then you have to tell. Yes?" Nora didn't plan on sharing anything of significance but agreed to play along.

For the next hour, Galina conveyed many personal stories having no problem admitting the errors made in her life. All those months in the same eight by twelve foot cell, and Nora had not been unaware of the sordid background lived by the middle-aged woman.

Once finished she asked, "Do you know what Galina means?" Nora shook her head. "God has redeemed."

After a few seconds of silence, Nora thanked her for being honest, but made no attempt to confess her own "sins," as Emma referred to them.

"Come now," said Galina, frustrated at having to work so hard to prompt a revelation of anything. "You must not be so perfect."

"Of course not." Nora said thinking of all her missteps. "I dropped out of my university and abandoned my brother in caring for our dying parents."

Her celly nodded, "Okay. What else?"

She tried not to be offended by Galina's light-hearted reaction to what had plagued Nora for years. "I refused to have any significant relationships."

Galina grinned. "Well, what boredom! Why not?"

Nora brought her knees up to her chest and rested her chin on them. No one could understand the fear of exposing her past mistakes. Galina picked up on her hesitation. "Come along."

"It doesn't matter." The doors clamored open for dinner.

Meal time was spent in silence while considering Emma's story. Afterwards Nora laid on her bed facing the wall as Galina gave her the emotional space she needed.

Unable to fall asleep, she mused about her cell mate and how much time they passed together. During their long talks, Nora only mentioned mundane blunders, never anything more. Certain things remained masked from everyone, including Michael and her parents. Bad choices too embarrassing and damaging to acknowledge were safer being hidden away: the decisions, the situations, and the guilt, all stuffed deep.

Maybe Galina and Tanya's therapists were right. Telling of the deepest shadows might be necessary to eliminate the power they held. Nora decided she would open up the following day. She dozed off anxious but with a sense of anticipated relief that finally someone else would know what she had kept concealed.

The women awoke the next morning when a guard clanged on their door to inform Galina that she was being moved to a facility in Dallas. Despite the protest, the yellow canvas bag was pushed through the bars and he said, "We move in ten. Get your crap together."

"How can they do this?" asked Nora helping to remove photographs of her celly's children from the walls.

"They can do anything," Galina said shoving her few possessions into the provided bag. "Be sure to find me, zhenshchina."

"Of course!" Although, neither suspected they would stay in touch.

The guard returned and they said goodbye before the door slammed closed and Nora fell into a funk while watching Galina being escorted away.

It took a full two weeks before Nora chose to tell her story and another five days to capture it.

Emma admitted surprise upon receiving Nora's correspondence. Enclosed in the envelope she found nine handwritten pages and she figured much soul searching and introspection had gone into the words. She curled up on her bed to read.

Dearest Emma.

Your experience is not silly nor insignificant as we all can learn from such experiences. I am honored that you trusted me with your secret. You were very brave to reveal it with me. Thank you for your enlightening story.

My apologies for the delayed response. Since we are being candid, I was not sure I wanted to divulge anything so intimate, however clearly it seems unfair not to do so. It took me awhile to put my words down on paper.

My story occurred when I was right around your age. I had been attending UT in Austin taking general studies and applied for and was accepted into Dell Medical School. Courses were to start five months later.

CHAPTER 61

TWENTY-EIGHT YEARS EARLIER

Nora was beyond ecstatic. She was going to med school! With trembling fingers she dialed the number of her parents' home.

"Guess what?" she said when her father answered the phone.

"What?"

"I got in!"

After a few moments of silence while her father composed himself, he managed, "I'm so proud of you, sweetie. When do you start?"

"In the fall semester."

"Well, should be enough time for a celebration."

"Dad, that isn't necessary."

"Nope, your mother and I already discussed it. If you got in, we'd throw a big party in your honor. Besides the weather's been nice, we could use a good excuse to relax."

Nora could forego the get-together, but hated to disappoint her father.

Fifteen days later she snuggled into her own bed back in the small town she grew up in. Her room hadn't changed at all with posters of Matt Dillon and Sean Penn tacked to the walls. *Sense and Sensibility*, *The Great Gatsby*, an *S.A.T. Study Guide*, and a collection of Jude Deveraux romance novels were arranged neatly on the shelves.

The March afternoon of the picnic was warmer than usual at eighty-seven degrees. The Collins' family and many of the old neighborhood friends sat under the Chinese pistache and Monterey oak trees. Like all the many picnics before, it was potluck style. Plenty of potato salad, baked beans, fresh strawberries, and sugar cookies lined the long tables. Nora's father and one of his long time coworkers, the high school baseball coach, braved the grill overflowing it with homemade burger patties. An oversized sign that Michael and his girlfriend had painted hung lopsided with ropes tied to the tree trunks.

CONGRATULATIONS, DR. COLLINS!

Everyone made the rounds to congratulate and wish Nora well. She didn't like all the extra attention and cringed with every hug given, but one look to her father's face caused her to smile and endure.

The old woman who lived across the street squeezed Nora's hand and went on and on talking about her great-grandchildren. "Uh-huh," Nora said, the neighbor clueless that she had lost her listener's attention. A periodic nod worked wonders.

At the edge of the park, Nora watched a young man unmount from a motorcycle. Her brother approached and slapped him on the back. They examined the shiny new bike, then walked towards Nora standing behind the great-grandmother. Michael opened and closed his fingers and Daniel made funny faces trying to make her laugh, but she held on. At long last, the woman noticed the boys standing behind her. "Oh, leave it to me talking your ear off. Sorry, my dear."

"Mrs. Cranston. Glad you're enjoying your grand-kids."

"Are you going to have children?"

Nora smiled, "Not for a while, yet. I'm starting school in a few months to be a physician."

"Oh, how lovely to hear. We could use a decent doctor in this town."

Nora wondered if the old woman even realized the whole reason for the gathering. She said goodbye and the lady turned, winked at the young men and walked away.

"Thanks for saving me. Gee Daniel, you're like an adult now." And he was. With pronounced biceps, a five o'clock shadow, and the silver braces missing from his teeth, he showed quite well. Too bad he was only finishing up his junior year in high school.

The boys had been best buddies since the third grade. By eleven, Daniel had developed a huge crush on Michael's older sister. Whenever he came over to their house, he couldn't take his eyes off her. She considered it sweet, remembering how she had drooled over her friends' older brothers when she was in middle school.

"Yup, an actual grown up person, now," Daniel said with a deep baritone voice followed up by a mischievous grin.

"Listen to you," exclaimed Nora noticing a twinkle in his green eyes and watching him shake back his wavy shoulder length hair.

Nora's mother came up, "Hi Daniel."

"Hey, Mrs. C. How are you?"

"Doing fine," she said slipping her hand through the crook of her daughter's arm. "Come say hello to the Bruins. They came all the way from Laredo to see you."

Nora obliged, planning to catch up with Daniel later. She peered back at him and he raised his hands saying, "Duty calls."

After a few hours, things wound down. Mothers began to wrap up leftovers handing them out to each other while fathers collected kids and sports equipment. The crowd thinned with comments like, "We've got to prepare for Sunday school," and "Science projects are due next week." Of course, that also prompted a whole new round of uncomfortable hugs for Nora.

The Collins' retained their record of being the last to leave the festivities. After everything was cleaned and packaged up, Nora and Michael informed their parents they planned on staying a while longer with some friends. Since Nora had driven her own car over, she could bring them both home. At seventeen and twenty-one, there were no issues.

She thanked her mother and father for everything. They told her again how happy and pleased they were about her future success. Her father threw the final box into the trunk. "Have fun, Dr. Collins."

Once the car disappeared around the corner, flasks appeared from Michael and Daniel's backpacks. The remaining three young ladies smiled.

Nora chuckled. "Is that what's wrong with you two? I figured you were up to your old tricks." Michael handed her the bronze container and she took a sip of the spicy Wild Turkey bourbon inside. She coughed and they all snickered.

"Don't drink much up at UT?" asked Daniel.

"Not this stuff."

The five friends talked, joked and reminisced of childhood stories growing up together, relating all the misbehavior when they were kids — yet Nora didn't have much to contribute.

"You were always the well-behaved one," Michael said.

"Not true," she defended herself. "Remember when I wrecked the car?"

He laughed. "Oh yeah, I forgot about that."

Nora always grappled with the apprehension of making a mistake and being ridiculed by somebody — most especially her father. Just two days after she received her driver's license she misjudged the distance needed to stop safely smashing the family Ford Escort into another car. Terrified to face her father, she sat on the curb shaking until the police called him. It was during football practice and she feared he'd be livid. He arrived on the scene as the broken glass was being swept into a pile at the side of the roadway. She stood as he rushed up to her, tears streamed down her cheeks. "I'm so sorry, Daddy."

Instead of being upset, he wiped her face, "Lesson learned?" She nodded then fell into his tight embrace until she stopped crying. Her mother had not been so understanding. Punishment? Cleaning out the refrigerator every week for two months.

Twilight brought cooler temperatures and the singing of cicadas. The two young women swore to drive up to Austin to get introduced to some cute fraternity boys. They giggled and left.

Michael, Nora and Daniel decided to run through McDonalds then head over to an old favorite hangout. She drove her and Michael while Daniel rode his motorcycle.

After parking, she found the flashlight in her glove compartment. They started along the overgrown pathway to the hidden spot. Michael glanced down to his watch, "Oh shit," he said. "I promised to go set up the gym for that special assembly on Monday morning."

"Can't you do it tomorrow?" asked Nora.

"No, I gotta go."

"We could come help you," she offered, although the last thing she wanted to do was go to another place to arrange chairs with a bunch of nosey adults.

"Nah, you go ahead. Can I use your car?" She relinquished her keys to Michael and told him to come back afterwards.

Off he went leaving Daniel and his sister alone. They pushed past the over grown brush until they found an old wooden picnic bench. He used a loose branch to sweep off twigs and leaves as best he could and they climbed atop the table resting their feet on the seat.

At first there was an unsettling quiet, then they heard it coming — the shrill whistle drawing closer and the rumble of the nearby tracks. Soon the ground and their bodies began to vibrate. They prepared as everyone privy to this covert location did by placing their hands over their ears and howling like dogs hearing ambulance sirens. The train roared by only twenty feet away on the other side of the bushes and the evidence trailed away into the night.

Daniel retrieved a bottle from his backpack. A pink agave worm on the bottom.

"I'm not drinking that," and she scrunched up her nose.

"McDonald's french fries always taste better with a little tequila. Something about the frying oil and the larva."

She swatted his arm and they laughed. Daniel had inherited a gift of gab from his mother and soon they had no shortage of chatter going on between them. As the full moon lit up the area, they devoured the greasy Big Mac and salty fries. Then each savored a sugary fried apple pie dessert. Nora licked the sticky cinnamon from her fingers and washed everything down with hefty amounts of tequila mixed in with her coke.

A couple of hours later, the two were undeniably relaxed. It felt so wonderful not to be worried about studying for exams or completing homework.

The temperature decreased to the mid-sixties and Nora shivered. From a zipper of the backpack, Daniel pulled out a black hooded sweatshirt with a small Arizona State University logo and gave it to her. She slipped it over her head, thankful for some reprieve from the chilly air. "You still carrying this thing around?"

"Of course. It's like a yellow post-it note on my forehead to remind me where I'm going after I get the hell out of this shitty bustling metropolis."

Nora laughed as she tightened the hood's drawstring and brushed the red devil embroidered on the shoulder. "This definitely fits you."

He cocked his head. "Got a 4.2 GPA."

"Impressive." She held up her cup and they toasted. "You get in, yet?"

"Applying next month."

She clasped her hands together inside the large center pocket. "Why ASU?"

He opened his arms wide. "My dad went there so what other options are there?" They laughed. "I do like their finance program, so it'll all work out. Pops will be happy and I'll make a shit-load of money. But maybe not as much as you being a doctor."

She smiled. Even though Daniel was younger, he acted much more mature than many of the men she had met. In fact, he impressed her with his knowledge on a host of topics including the supposed free market system, the conspiracy behind the creation of the Federal Reserve, the increasing craze of ordering books via the computer from some company called Amazon, and Daniel's laments over the recent death of sports announcer, Howard Cosell.

How had Daniel got so smart? had been Nora's last comprehended thought. She didn't remember who kissed who first, or who initiated what. All she knew was that there came a jumble of pleasant activity.

"Nora, wake up. Come on, wake up." Michael shook her.

Lying on top of the wood table, her legs were curled into the black sweatshirt. Her eyes half opened as she tried focusing on her brother. "Mikey," she slurred, smiling. "You came back."

"How much did you guys drink?"

He grimaced at his friend passed out against a tree, bare chested and no shoes. "What happened?" he kicked his friends foot, but he didn't budge.

"I was cold. I'm cold, Mikey," said Nora as he helped her up and they stumbled past Daniel. "He ate the worm. Can you believe it?"

With his arm around her waist, Michael half-carried and half-guided his inebriated sister to the car and laid her down across the back seat. "I'll tell Mom and Dad you spent the night with Katie. They'll totally have a cow if they see you so shit-faced."

"What about Daniel?" Nora asked.

"He can sleep it off here," said Michael.

As you said in your letter, Emma, things happen. That they did and my grave error in judgment soon revealed itself.

CHAPTER 62

Emma straightened out her left leg that had been tucked under her. It had fallen asleep. She turned to the next of many handwritten pages.

NORA'S LETTER TO EMMA CONTINUED

At dawn, several unusual horn blasts from a train jolted me awake, but soon I was sleeping again in the backseat of my car. The next morning the news reported the sheriff had pulled what was left of Daniel's body from the railroad tracks. Because of the alcohol found in his bloodstream, they assumed he wandered in front of the engine in a drunken stupor. Neither Michael nor I told anyone about being there with Daniel the night before.

Even though physically I knew what had transpired, mentally I refused to admit making love with that boy — until six weeks later when I awoke with the urge to vomit.

I became so conflicted because I always wanted children — but not quite yet. With so much I still wanted to do, completing my education seemed so important. It was inconceivable to imagine having a baby from an under-aged and deceased boy. No one found out what Daniel and I had done for I would have been blamed for everything. The residing secret ours — well, mine.

I made my decision on the second of June (which happens to also be Toby Martinez' postponement date many years later), and terminated the pregnancy. If I could just fix the problem caused by my mistake, things would go back to normal. Little did I understand that for me, a whole slew of new problems would arise.

Not wanting to be recognized, I scheduled with a clinic in another city. The procedure was difficult for me and I experienced complications after the abortion. My cervix was damaged causing an acute infection. In a foolish way, I justified it as what I deserved.

I returned to classes pretending everything was the same as the day before — but it wasn't. It wasn't okay. Just because something is legal, it doesn't guarantee there will not be consequences. The ironic thing, Emma, is that even if Daniel would not have died or if the postponing option was available back then, I'm not sure I would have chosen any differently.

Everything shifted as I started down a path filled with the inability to see anything through. I stopped going to visit my parents because being around them reminded me of how I'd let everyone down when I quit school and did not return. I was once a daughter who was to become a doctor. Now I was a college drop out. How I had crushed their hearts.

When things got serious with a man, I found a reason to end it. I ceased dating all together when I hit thirty convincing myself that I never could bear children, though nobody ever gave me that diagnosis. Unlovable and naive, I know.

As I spiraled downwards, I abandoned the responsibility for my aging parents to my brother. They went to their graves never understanding any of my irrational behavior.

Holding down a job was hopeless and I bounced from employer to employer and moved from state to state trying to discover what I should do with my messed up life. There's no need to bore you with all the other stupid things I've done.

Most of the time I force myself to not think about all my poor choices ensuring they remain packed away. Nevertheless, they do manifest themselves in sub-conscious ways like withdrawing from those who care about me. I developed an eating disorder for a while. I drank too much, perhaps still do — except for in here. For years I struggled with loneliness, isolation and insomnia. Some time ago, I took up running several miles a day for something else to focus on and to exhaust myself enough to fall asleep.

I stayed with TPC solely because I gained the most comfort and connection being in the presence of those postponed babies. They did not judge me. Perhaps it grew into a type of catharsis.

Those things we try to escape, do bubble up to haunt us periodically. They seep their way back into our thoughts and we relive them, hating ourselves all over again. We suffer from the results of bad momentary decisions. If fortunate, life and the distance of time keeps these errors out of our conscious to avoid experiencing their wretched ache.

Finding clarity is something we all seek from our past actions. Justification is simple. Dealing with penitence is not and grief is easier to let go of than guilt. It isn't that I don't need to deal with my mistakes, I simply don't know how. If only I had done something different. I can't forgive myself because it's impossible to go back and change what happened.

The last week has been hard for me, Emma. I had to process feelings I never wanted to wrestle with. Ones that I had kept under a veil of suppression for decades. It was like climbing aboard a roller coaster ride of emotions tearing from disappointment to pain to remorse to shame and sadness. A heart-wrenching exercise.

But you compelled me to break my silence, so perhaps by some miracle, I might begin to heal. Thank you for that, Emma. Will I ever not regret some of the choices I made? Probably not. I'm not very good at forgiveness.
    Your trusted and grateful friend.
    Nora.

    Emma dabbed at her watery eyes. Nora had indeed opened up her heart and soul and Emma was saddened and honored.

CHAPTER 63

The act of exchanging letters with Emma began to open up Nora's mind. She found herself feeling freer and lighter than ever before enabling her to acknowledge and accept her mistakes. To put thoughts and words to all her decisions allowed for the healing from old scars and deep regrets.

Imagination flowed and after years of failure in starting to write a children's book, the blocks fell away. Her day and night dreams filled with ideas about Toby and all the other sleeping neonates — the children whose lives she had touched.

She assumed her first story would be about the boy she risked everything for. But early one morning upon finding her face wet, she realized it must be about the child with whom Toby shared a special date.

Nora had never given her and Daniel's lost baby a name, but now came the moment. She sensed it to have been a girl. After some consideration, she called her Galina — God has redeemed. The first of many tears were wiped away as she picked up a pen and began writing.

"Once a little girl named Galina sat on top of a park bench surrounded by beautiful trees. Long golden curls bounced around her face when she giggled. Her grassy green eyes were wide with wonder. Galina enjoyed many friends but her favorite person in the whole world was her father. He was such a handsome man with wavy dark hair that hung to his shoulders. He was the conductor on a train and she traveled with him to exotic places like —"

After serving twelve months, Nora was released from prison and accepted a part-time position as a copywriter for an online website catering to parents. She worked from home researching and creating articles dealing with child-rearing — quite interesting being she had never had children of her own. She used a pseudonym. A move to a small town outside of San Antonio kept her from a lot of eyeballs and questions about her history.

Nora did not tell Michael about her experience with Daniel. Maybe someday she would tell him, if the time was right.

CHAPTER 64

TWENTY-TWO YEARS LATER

Nora finished her first novel while in jail and titled it, *My Time - Galina*. For the next twenty-two years, she wrote for children. Lined up across the bookshelves in her living room were dusty reference texts: *Publishing Children's Books*, *Structuring and Writing a Book Series*, and a well-used and dog-eared book called *Creating Stories Kids Will Love*.

A long string of colorful books leaned against each other. The spines revealing the titles: *My Time - Galina*, *My Time - Toby*, *My Time - Stephany*. The series expanded with *Thomas*, *Missy*, *Brandon*, *Annie*, and even, *Cole*.

She still utilized the pen name, NP Casey, and was working on her twenty-sixth novel. Her written work had become successful and made the young adult reading lists, both domestic and international. Her reputation of being a reclusive author led to her rejecting every opportunity to speak or participate at new release signings. Her prose happened not for money, but to get the stories out of her head.

Nora's novels told how the children's lives postponed at TPC might have gone. All grand adventures, harrowing circumstances, side-splitting humor, longed-for joy, and how the children overcame adversities. Challenges every child must face was wrapped inside a wild and stupendous journey where kids were the heroes because of their unique personalities.

She sensed a closeness with all her protagonists, just as with the little lives in Crypod Holding. All their tales had been created vividly in Nora's imagination. Never did she attempt to find out what really happened to any of the babies, including Toby.

Her modest three bedroom home sat on an acre of land with enough space between the houses where neighbors didn't get into each other's business. She preferred being out of the hustle and bustle of the city. The house was paid for and she kept to herself, rarely venturing out.

Spring brought a warm breeze that filled the air with the fresh, pungent aroma of brilliant yellow and purple petunias. She bordered the eight by eight foot covered patio space with potted plants and flowers. Quiet instrumental music came from an outdoor speaker while a nearby fountain splashed and gurgled — a sound she always found comforting because it reminded her of the crypods.

Within her constructed inspirational sanctuary, Nora spent countless hours constructing her writing. Her favorite part of the space was the proximity to the local elementary school.

It was near enough to see the children playing, hear their laughing, listen to their arguing, and witness the fear of some to slip down the slide and the insecurities of the bullies that ridiculed them. She observed the loners and the outgoing ones; those that sought any type of attention by breaking the rules and getting in trouble and bigger children that picked up the smaller ones after taking a tumble and brushing off their scrapped elbows. Nora came up with all their names and monitored them for hours and literally years as she developed her narrations.

On the wicker table in front of her lay the most recent letter from Emma awaiting a reply. Neither woman ever suggested they come together in person, but they continued to correspond, staying abreast of what was happening in each other's worlds. She celebrated from afar when Emma graduated with a master's degree in social psychology, accepted a position in New York City, met and married a man, and bore three children, the first who was about to enter an ivy-league university. All had been done with no postponement, but with a nanny, for sure. The woman, almost thirty years her junior, ended up more of a friend than anyone else.

Nora sat in her padded lounge chair flipping pages in a hefty stack of papers. She made circles and jotted notes with a red marker. Her hair was completely gray and prominent lines embellished her face.

A chime came from the front door. The neighborhood handy-man had installed a secondary bell making it audible outside. "About time," she muttered and climbed to her feet. Emma would call it "old school," but Nora still liked to read her book drafts in hard copy. The office supply store messed up her print cartridge and paper order the first time by sending it to Tennessee instead of Texas. With an apology, they promised to re-send it at no charge.

The doorbell dinged again as Nora dropped the manuscript to the table and walked to her front door. "Coming!" she called out. She was a little slower due to aging knees. Thirty years of running had caught up to her a few years back and the arthritis in those knee joints flared up on occasion. Ordering supplies, groceries and virtually everything else for home delivery meant for fewer steps.

Nora pushed on the door to unlock the deadbolt recognizing some day she would need to call the handyman back to repair that along with some other annoying things. She swung the door open and saw a young man with a mop of dark curly hair and dimples in his cheeks.

CHAPTER 65

Nora smiled at the young man standing at her front door. "Hello there."

"Nora Collins?" he asked.

She wondered about the missing boxes. "That's me."

He stared at her for a moment. "I'm Toby Martinez."

Light-headedness caused Nora to grasp the door frame and she could do nothing but stare at him. Could this be that precious little boy standing in front of her, not in a wheelchair like she had envisioned in her book.

"I wanted to meet you. You cool with that?" Flushed and shaky, Nora managed a smile and nodded. He stepped inside and she motioned him down the hall.

She walked behind him observing a moderate limp, but walking nonetheless. Nora clenched her hands together to hide her trembling. "Would you like something to drink?"

"No, that's okay."

Toby sat down near the edge of the couch while Nora got herself into a chair still unable to take her eyes off him. He perused the room then back down to his legs, removing imaginary lint off his jeans.

Struggling, she at last found some words. "So, you grew up."

"Yup," he said tapping his hands on the sofa. "Turned twenty-two a couple months back."

She nodded, although she already knew it had been his birthday. Every single year, six months before his legal birthday and on what she considered his real birthday — the second of June, she baked and enjoyed sprinkle cupcakes. "Has it been that long?" After an awkward silence, Nora blurted out, "I'm sorry I couldn't have done more."

Toby's face lit up with a bright smile. "Hang-on a second." He walked back to her front door. Maybe he was fetching an old photo album. Isn't that what people did in these types of situations? But no one had been in that situation before, besides, people kept everything on their personal devices those days.

Sixty seconds later, Toby reentered the room stepping back to reveal a young woman holding a girl about two years old. "This is my wife, Cindy and our daughter, Bridgette." His voice reflecting his pride.

Floored again, she rose to greet Cindy. As she touched the tender skin of Bridgette's hand, the little girl pulled back with caution. "She's beautiful," said Nora noting the head full of dark hair like her father.

They all sat down. Bridgette clung to her mother while maintaining a wary eye glued on the stranger. With a death grip she held a doll wearing a frilly pink dress.

"What's your doll's name?" Nora smiled at the girl who wedged herself hard between the cushions and Cindy's arm. Beginning to feel overwhelmed, Nora took a deep breath, turned back to Toby and asked, "Are you going to college?"

"I am," he replied. "Turned out I found learning easy so excelled fast and now I'm in my second semester of law school at UT up in Austin."

"Very nice and my alma mater. How are your parents?"

"Doing well. I have a younger sister too, she's fifteen now." Nora's eyes unintentionally glanced at Toby's legs. She didn't mean to do it but she appreciated his graciousness. "She's running cross country at her high school."

Nora exhaled, looking at Cindy. "I was so grateful they didn't press charges when all that stuff happened."

"Yeah," said Toby. "Sounds like my mom was freaked out, but my dad convinced her to let things go. Him and Aunt Erin."

"Erin?"

"Well, she's not my real aunt. I think you knew her when I was a baby. She's a close friend of the family."

She swallowed hard as Toby's daughter relaxed, parked herself on the hardwood floor and using her fingers began combing her doll's long hair. "We lost touch," Nora said skipping the more accurate explanation.

"When Toby was twelve, his parents told him what happened," said Cindy.

"Yeah, it wasn't new about being a postponement baby because people would make comments to me once in a while. But I had no idea about everything else," added Toby.

"Were you ever teased by other kids about being postponed?" Nora asked, curious to see if that part of the made-up story of his life was as inaccurate as her mental image was turning out to be.

He laughed. "I endured my fair share of torment, but not because of that, because of these." He tapped on his thighs. Guess that was to be expected." She had been right about the teasing.

"Kids are so mean," Cindy said. Nora could attest to that truth, never mind what year it was or what age children were. She viewed it daily with those on the playground. Their gazes fell to Bridgette who began singing contentedly to herself. Her dimples identical to Toby's.

"I figure we all have adversity and must find a way to face it. It makes us who we are," Toby said. Warmth spread across Nora's chest. "Actually, I wanted to thank you for being so brave and for remaining true to your convictions. Aunt Erin said thanks to you, I'm much better off than I would have been."

"I don't know —"

"No really," he interrupted. "The technology came out about a year after I was born and it only supposedly worked on kids under two. She said I would have been in a chair." Nora fought the emotions that began creeping in. "Plus, I probably wouldn't have these two." Toby rubbed his wife's shoulders and patted the top of his daughter's bobbing head.

"I remember watching you almost every day in your crypod. Just lying there, perfectly still. Unaware of all that was going on around you." Her eyes glistened in remembrance. "My boss was always giving me the evil eye."

They all laughed easing the tension.

"Well, my dad said the head guy was forced to resign but not before the company negotiated a long-term settlement with my parents."

"Good for them," Nora said.

"So," Toby began, hesitating before continuing. "My mom doesn't know we're here. My father was the one who encouraged me to come. He made me promise not to tell her."

Nora raised her eyebrows and made a zipping motion across her lips and a moment of silence passed. Still despite how things had turned out, Sylvia stayed upset with her.

Toby noticed the thick manuscript and a printed article entitled *Editing With the Axe of Love*, on the coffee table. "You a writer?"

"Oh, I dabble a bit," she said not looking to the bookcase with all her accomplishments.

They chatted for the next half hour about various topics. Nora and Toby each swapped turns answering the other's inquiries into his growing up and her ordeal in taking and keeping him for five months.

He consulted his cell phone for the time. She didn't want him to leave even though she felt emotionally exhausted and ready for a glass of wine. "Are you sure I can't get you some water or something? I'd be happy to throw together some sandwiches or —"

"Well, we need to get back up to Austin," he said and stood. Cindy scooped up Bridgette and Nora rose to her feet. "There is this big ethics paper I have to finish."

Nora grinned, "About postponement?"

Toby chuckled and waved off her comment in a playful manner as they all headed to the door. "Nah, not controversial enough. It's on synthetic food sources."

Cindy turned back. "So great meeting you, Nora."

"It was a pleasure meeting you as well, Cindy." Then she reached out and brushed the little girl's silken chin. "Bye-bye, sweet Bridgette." A giggle emerged before Bridgette buried her face in her mother's shoulder.

The mother carried the child out and down the walkway leaving Toby and Nora to have their final words.

"I appreciate you coming."

"Of course. It was great to finally see what you looked like other than footage from those old news reports."

"That was a long time ago," she said and put her hand on his shoulder. "I'm so impressed with you, Toby Martinez."

He smiled back, then unexpectedly gave her a sincere hug. She squeezed him tight feeling his firm, strong body matured from the tiny helpless one she had sponged off in that dank motel room so long ago. Toby stopped the embrace first though she wanted to keep ahold of this intelligent young man. He walked away without making eye-contact and she speculated he had also teared up.

"Will you come again? Bring your family."

He stared out at the street. "Well, school's kind of busy and I've got this part time job that —" A small smile appeared. "I'll try."

"That would be wonderful," she said. "I can fix my famous spaghetti. Mushy pasta and all."

Toby laughed, "Deal." He limped to a brand new reflective sky-blue SUV where his wife and child sat strapped in and ready to go. Happy with his new ride, he turned, opened his arms wide and called out, "Courtesy of your ex-employer."

Nora nodded in acknowledgement. He got in but didn't close the door, rather he jumped back out and returned to hand her a paper sack. "I almost forgot. My dad asked me to give this to you."

"Thank you," she said without looking inside. Then with a wave, He was gone.

She closed the front door and withdrew from the bag the black ASU sweatshirt. The one Daniel had lent her the night before he died. The one she wore while evading the police for five months. And the one she bundled Toby in the night he reanimated.

An envelope was tucked in the sleeve and she opened it to find some of Toby's childhood photographs and a short handwritten note.

Dear Nora, I kept this shirt hidden away in the back of my closet hoping someday I could return it to you. I know you always wanted the best for Toby and as you can see, he turned out to be quite a special young man. I believe you had something to do with that. Thank you. Sincerely, Ruben Martinez.

Nora used a tissue from her pocket to wipe her eyes as she walked in the kitchen to uncork a new bottle of blackberry wine. Michael had gone into partnership with his winemaker friend and kept her with an ample supply. As the deep rich liquid filled her glass, she began to feel an odd sense of peace with all that happened so long ago.

Her phone rang and it startled her. Michael's face displayed on the screen and she allowed the call to go to voice mail not wanting to be stolen from that glorious moment quite yet.

Carrying her glass and the bottle out to the safety of her back porch, she settled into her well used chair. She gazed to the deserted playground. Classes were still in session, but soon the children would emerge to flood the sandboxes, swings, merry-go-round and tetherball courts.

After the familiar notification toned, she listened to Michael's message. "Hey Nora Bora. So in exemplary sisterly fashion, you never pick up. I wanted to remind you of the Fourth of July barbecue." Not a year went by without his invitation to this event. "Everyone's going to be there so you should come. I'm providing you plenty of notice so you can't say no. Oh and there's a couple old bachelors coming. One's pretty damn good looking for eighty-two! Call me back — please."

She laughed and hit delete on the phone. *He was a kind-hearted brother*, she thought. Even though he made her nuts sometimes, he still cared about her. Nora toyed with the idea of attending the picnic that summer. Maybe.

Time changed Nora's perspective about her own parents. In her gut she knew they never condemned nor loved her any less because she quit school or didn't come home often. In fact, they would have forgiven her for all her misdeeds and bad choices and even about going to prison. They only wanted her presence, yet in reality she had been mostly absent. These were experiences not to be proud of, but just to accept.

The buzzer sounded and in two minutes the students sprinted to the play area. Little people hung from the monkey bars and pumped on the swing set.

Nora spotted the young boy she had watched for the past six years. Now in sixth grade, in the fall he would attend the middle school three miles down the road. She remembered seeing him for the first time in kindergarten when he set his small wheelchair on the basketball court and tried to shoot hoops.

She had witnessed anguish and laughter, but this confident boy was always back the next day. He didn't allow his inability to run stop him. Sitting near the bottom of the slide, he yelled out encouragements to the youngest boys and girls who were afraid to come down. He smiled and laughed and was included in the group as a part of all the other children. It became apparent that he was well-liked and lacked nothing. A tear escaped, rolled down her cheek and plopped into her glass.

Though she experienced a certain amount of remorse with all that happened with Toby, she felt peaceful about her actions knowing she played at least a small part in his life. By influencing Ruben and Sylvia to wait long beyond when they wanted to bring him home, she had made a difference, albeit not perfect. If taken earlier, he would for sure have not been able to walk and have many physical challenges and defeats. Yet now he had a wife and daughter of his own. She never imagined he would give her the gift of a visit.

Nora understood she had been wrong to assume Toby would not have lived a full life, one bursting with possibility. One abundant with happiness and loving parents and siblings regardless of a wheelchair, braces, limps or anything else. A life where people helped you and loved you no matter your physical or psychological struggles. And most important, forgave you for all your mistakes.

Thank you for embarking on the journey within the pages of *Postponement*. Your time and dedication to this story means the world to me. If you found inspiration, insight or enjoyed the book, I would be deeply grateful if you could take a moment to share your thoughts with others. Your review and/or rating can make a significant impact and is a testament to the power of storytelling.

Please consider leaving an honest review on platforms like Amazon, Goodreads, BookBub, or wherever you acquired your copy of the book. Your feedback, no matter how brief, is immensely valuable and much appreciated as it helps people discover meaningful stories.

Thanks again for being a part of this literary adventure. I'm excited to hear your reactions on *Postponement*.

Warm regards,
Diane

ABOUT THE AUTHOR

Diane has long been a lover of storytelling. She began her path down the world of sharing her stories in novels upon an unexpected move from Phoenix to Texas for 6 years. Now settled back in Phoenix, she continues to write. Diane also is passionate about independent filmmaking that offers her the opportunity to share her stories on film as well. She has written, directed and/or produced a feature film and several short films winning numerous awards for her efforts including receiving the 2012 Arizona Filmmaker of the Year Award.

Diane spent 27 years in corporate Human Resources and Training with most of that time in management and executive level positions in the financial and travel industries. She holds a Masters degree in Adult Education and a Bachelors degree in Human Services.

Author & Blog Website: www.dianedresback.com
Filmmaking Website: www.mindclover.com

A Note from Diane:

Thank you for taking the Postponement journey! I would love to hear from you so feel free to be in touch! I would be honored to have you in my readers email group which allows me to let you know when I have news or new books and importantly giveaways and discounts. You can sign up at my websites: www.dianedresback.com.

BOOKS BY DIANE M. DRESBACK

FICTION

Awake As A Stranger trilogy
...*Awakening* (Book 1)
...*Rebellion* (Book 2)
...*Altercation* (Book 3)
Treaz and Omani reside on two different continents yet each are trapped in deplorable realities—Treaz living within other people's bodies and Omani being held captive on her uncle's compound. Both long to regain control over their lives, escape their merciless captors, and expose the haunting truths facing them and the world. Can they find freedom together?

Postponement
Technology allows for the delay of parenthood by cryo-suspension of newborns. Nora Collins navigates an ethical minefield and risks everything for one infant.

Reminisce
If your memories make you who you are, then what happens when you change them? Nick discovers a world of drug-induced memory manipulation in order to overcome his struggles.

Promise of Protection
What if YOU held the power to manipulate the well-being or the demise of many? Joe is called to a senior living facility 16 hours away. He unwillingly becomes entangled in unraveling the bizarre scientific work of his estranged father.

Room For Another: A Courageous Adoption Story Based on True Events
Every choice carries a consequence. After the death of her mother, an unloving stepmother, and an uninvolved father, Theresa must deal with another trauma—an unwanted pregnancy.

NON-FICTION

From Us For You: Inspiring Stories of Healing, Growth and Transformation
25 inspiring stories of healing, growth and transformation compiled from women and meant to encourage and inspire readers. Net-profits of book sales are donated to a nonprofit advocating for and assisting in the needs of women.

Your Action, Your Success: Motivating Yourself To Get Things Done
What stops you from getting more done? Fear? Time? Procrastination? This book offers easy, no-nonsense tips and strategies to help yourself get more things accomplished.

To find out more or purchase any of these books, please visit www.dianedresback.com

Printed in Great Britain
by Amazon